THE CASE
A HISTORICAL NOVEL — A TRUE STORY

A Novel by Tsuriel Sdomi

Producer & International Distributor
eBookPro Publishing
www.ebook-pro.com

THE CASE OF THE GERMAN DOCTOR: A HISTORICAL
NOVEL BASED ON A TRUE STORY
Tsuriel Sdomi

Copyright © 2023 Tsuriel Sdomi

All rights reserved; No parts of this book may be
reproduced or transmitted in any form or by any means,
electronic or mechanical, including photocopying,
recording, taping, or by any information retrieval system,
without the permission, in writing, of the author.

Translation: Yardenne Greenspan
Editing: Matthew Berman
Contact: ori1060@gmail.com

ISBN 9798856664033

THE CASE OF THE GERMAN DOCTOR:

A Historical Novel Based on a True Story

A NOVEL BY TSURIEL SDOMI

Dr. William Ludwig von Antrim was born in a wealthy suburb of Munich, a descendent of a long-standing dynasty, an educated mélange of sturdy German-Merovingian nobility that branched into a gentle Carolingian heritage. There was blue blood, an aristocratic inheritance of a faulty hemophilic gene, and old money. Many of his relatives had served as diplomats, consuls, or confidants to the high and mighty. A few grew to become bold generals or sleepy Bundestag ministers. As an only son, William was destined, one day, to join his kin in carrying the hefty burden of public service.

His childhood memories began at age four, at the expansive family mansion that sprawled over green lawns above the Bodensee Lake. The clouds of war were still light and white, floating languidly over a peaceful Bavarian landscape.

The house was an Italian villa designed in Palladian style, with marble columns in the façade, a pediment coated with Greek relief, and a long avenue of linden trees leading from the gates to the horseshoe driveway in front of the house. There, his grandfather had erected a marble fountain adorned with mischievous water elves dancing around a buxom goddess of fertility, who was trapped in the muscular embrace of a horned satyr with an erection and a malicious smile.

In spite of his misleading Nordic looks—straight blond hair, blue eyes, slanted nose—the Gestapo discovered that Jewish blood flowed through William's mother's veins. No one knew for certain how this shameful information had come to light, or on the basis of what evidence. But one thing was beyond all doubt—when the Gestapo broke into the civilian archive in Berlin, Eva's name made it onto a list of suspected communists, members of the Kreisau Circle, and Jewish magnates who had smuggled their capital abroad ahead of time and fled the country just before the annexation of Austria.

From this point on, things happened at a dizzying speed. An anonymous warning letter was sent to William's father, who worked at the Department of Racial Purity at the Berlin Ministry of Interiors. The letter was laconic and signed illegibly by someone who had introduced himself as a friend of the family. The motives for keeping his identity a secret needed no explanation. He offered an escape plan, but time was of the essence. William's father's hand trembled as he read the letter.

Their parting was brief and charged with pent-up emotions. William wrapped his small arms around his father's neck, leaned his soft cheek against his father's rough one, and sobbed. The cool aroma of cologne and pungent pipe smoke would become his last memory of the man.

That same night, William and his mother crossed the border to Switzerland, along with his nanny, his father's personal secretary, and a burly Serbian bodyguard. They arrived in Napoli around midnight the following day, and from there sailed to America on a Greek merchant ship that left the port with its lights dimmed. Three weeks later, they docked at Ellis Island. They shoved their way onto the platform along with tens of thousands of other Jewish refugees—a long human stream that slowly made its way to the immigrant station, one step at a time.

William watched the other people curiously. Years later, he would admit that this was the first time he'd ever seen Jews, and no, he hadn't felt the echoing of their shared blood, or the mute cry of a mutual ancestor. He felt nothing but childish curiosity. In the tight expressions of the children, he found a combination of innocence and perilous animalistic vitality. They looked at him askance, examining him indifferently from the corners of their eyes. They spent hours sitting on a heap of tattered leather suitcases tied with ropes, wearing old wool suits, matchstick legs dangling back and forth.

Three people in suits waited for them by the check-in counter and led them down long hallways to a side room for questioning and passport control. From there, they were taken to the infirmary. A young military doctor listened to William's heart and checked his teeth and ears. In flawless German, the doctor asked William's mother about any childhood illnesses and vaccinations. It was all done cheerfully, almost offhand.

From the island, they were transported to an apartment that had been issued to them ahead of time. The spacious apartment was on 24th Street in Brooklyn, near a playground and a small shopping center. A generous stipend was deposited in their bank account each month. An Austrian Consulate employee who introduced himself as Oscar told Eva over the phone that he would be taking care of all their future needs. He insinuated that they'd known each other a long time, but graciously turned down her offer to meet in person.

Eva furnished the apartment in an old-fashioned style: heavy wooden furniture, crystal chandeliers, and oriental rugs. The walls were decorated with paintings by Liebermann, Baurenfeind, and Emil Nolde. Soft sonatas by Brahms and Schumann filled the apartment while right outside the door New York went on sizzling.

William had a strict schedule. "The war will be over in a month or two," his mother told the nanny. "We must maintain our old routine in order to spare the child any unnecessary emotional tumult."

They spoke German and French at home. When he went to the playground, the nanny watched like a hawk to make sure he didn't fraternize with any American children, whom she referred to as "rude and unmannered."

They first heard from the Immigration Department three months after arriving in the United States. Oscar instructed William's mother to start using her maiden name again before the appointment, but Eva refused vehemently. "I'm not going to change my last name."

"It's only temporary," Oscar pleaded. "The name Wittgenstein sounds Jewish. I'm afraid that the name von Antrim might cause you needless trouble."

Oscar's advice was valid. German and Japanese immigrant applications for American citizenships were handled with the utmost care, if not with blatant suspicion. The candidates were required to bring written support for their claims and sign declarations of loyalty. These demands were often accompanied by surveillance, tapped phones, and humiliating interrogations by federal agents.

Declaring her Jewish faith to the Bureau of Population, Refugees, and Migration was the first step in Eva's naturalization process. In a tailored blue suit and legs crossed to the side, Eva faced the committee members, introducing herself in third person with a heavy German accent. "Ms. Wittgenstein, Jewish refugee from Germany, of reasonable financial means, but entirely helpless." She emanated a feminine despair, an outwardly sexual plasma with the intent to awaken the agents' protective masculine instinct. It did the trick. The three men on the committee smiled at her affectionately, nodding along as she spoke, encouraging her with hungry looks. The two older women on the committee watched her with crooked smiles, their heads bobbing in broken motions. Inching toward the end of menopause, the two pricked up their narrow rat-like noses, suspiciously sniffing for the lustful scent of an abandoned uterus. They gave the heartbreaking depositions a careful read but believed not a single word of them. They barked their questions at her with contempt.

"Who said you were Jewish?"

"The Gestapo."

"The Gestapo?"

"Yes. The Gestapo sent my husband a letter, explaining that according to records found in the civilian archive in Berlin, I am of Jewish descent."

"But you yourself were not aware of this?"

"My parents hid my Jewish identity from me. They were absolute atheists."

"Do you have any documents confirming your Jewish identity?"

"No. They were lost when the archive was set on fire."

The women glanced at each other meaningfully but said nothing.

One of the men asked, "Do you live by the edicts of Jewish faith?"

"I'm Jewish, but I'm not religious."

"And your husband?"

"He's an atheist."

"And where is he now?"

"I don't know."

"What do you mean you don't know?"

"I haven't heard from him since I got here."

The women scribbled in their notepads furiously, the older one looking up severely at Eva as she wrote. "That's enough for now. You can go. A decision will arrive by mail."

The women's conclusion was clear: a beautiful, educated woman with millions of dollars' worth of assets who had managed to flee Germany without losing a single hair off her head had to be a manipulative, cold-blooded, stone-hearted bitch. They were prepared to believe any theory attesting to her being evil, contemptible, even cruel. As far as they were concerned, she could just as easily have been a Nazi spy. They questioned her Jewish origins.

Her own body seemed to disprove her claims. The high cheekbones, the slanted blue eyes, the pearly white skin, and blond hair—they all attested to irrefutable Teutonic genes. Couple these with her erect stance and the tyrannical gaze that emerged from her eyes whenever one of the men caught her glance, and you've got yourself a standard Nazi bitch. The women spoke their piece, but were overtaken by a crushing male majority.

Her application was approved on the spot.

The appointment had been preceded by sleepless nights spent standing in front of the bathroom mirror, naked as the day she was born, examining her body from every direction. The straight nose, the properly molded skull, the blue eyes—they all seemed intact and perfectly Aryan. Who could have played such a devilish trick on her? And as punishment for what sin?

She couldn't come up with any misdeeds she'd committed. Of course, there was that embarrassing incident with her childhood friend Paulina von Herberts. The von Herberts' mansion, built on a three-hundred-acre tract, bordered Eva's parents' modest property, and the two families had a close relationship. But that unfortunate event had taken place years ago, long before her Jewish identity had been revealed. Besides, it hadn't been her fault.

On a day off from school, she and her friend went on a shopping trip to Munich. As they walked out of a café on Marienplatz, they were detained by Gestapo soldiers on a recon tour. The soldiers only asked Paulina for her papers.

Paulina, with her soft, Semitic features and wavy black hair, shivered with fear, but more so with rage and humiliation. Passersby began to gather around. Voice shaking, the only daughter of the consul and Bundestag member, von Herberts and a Milanese *contessa* mumbled over and over again, "*Ich bin Deutsche.*"

Unimpressed with her words, the soldiers carefully reviewed her papers, shifting their watchful eyes back and forth from her face to the photograph. Finally, without a word of apology, they gave back her identification card and took off, while onlookers continued to eye the crying girl with hostile suspicion.

They asked Eva for nothing. On the contrary—they smiled at her flirtatiously. To them, she was Aryan beyond all doubt. As they were leaving, the youngest among them turned back and winked at her, smiling mischievously and waving an enthusiastic goodbye.

On the train ride home, Paulina ensconced herself in silence. Every once in a while, she pulled a small silk handkerchief from her pocket and dried her tears on it. All of Eva's attempts at comforting her were rebuffed.

The next day, when Eva called Paulina at home, the housekeeper informed her that the young miss was no longer interested in their friendship. At university, Paulina ignored Eva. Ultimately, Eva stopped trying.

These days, she asked herself if Paulina had known Eva was Jewish even then. Did she laugh and gloat years later, upon hearing how Eva had been forced to scurry away like a mouse? Eva had never felt so humiliated in her life. The shame, the guilt, and the loneliness devastated her.

One night, little William woke up, got out of bed and followed his mother as she stumbled, drunk, into the bathroom. Through a crack in the door, he saw her standing in front of the mirror in the moonlight, wearing a thin silk nightgown, her face flushed and damp, eyes closed. Her fingers combed through her sweat-drenched hair, fluttered over her chest and stomach, then down into her inner thighs. Her lips murmured affectionate words in German.

Suddenly, blood began to run between her legs. She opened her eyes with fright, sent searching fingers over to her crotch, and then held them, bloody, to her face, fuming. "Whore. Dirty Jew, filthy Jew, dirty slut."

A terrified William fled back to his bedroom.

The next morning, at breakfast, he whispered the words he'd heard to himself. His mother, who had been sitting beside him, buttering a piece of toast, lost in thought, froze. The knife fell from her hand. Then she whipped her body in his direction and slapped him, hard. His cup of cocoa slipped from his grip and shattered on the floor.

William lowered his head, but no sound came from his pursed lips. Stunned by her savage violence and the uncovering of her shameful secret, she pulled him into her arms and wept.

She abhorred the representatives of the Jewish community who came by her apartment to ask how they could be of assistance. Their mere existence was sufficient to wreck her good old world and render her a refugee against her will. Had it not been for them, for their mortifying presence in her blood and golden genes, she would have still been living with her family on the banks of the Bodensee.

When they addressed her in Yiddish, she spat at them in German: "*Ich spreche nur Deutsch.*"

That settled it. Hitler, Goebbels, and Göring's animalistic German had uprooted their lives and still haunted their sleep. All of them, down to the last one, left large families behind in the old homeland—families who were murdered in extermination camps. Fathers, mothers, brothers, sisters, aunts, uncles, and cousins. The cutting German in her mouth was a testimony, a memento of evil.

They were fluent in German. They admired the language. Who among their generation's American writers could hold a candle to Goethe, Schiller, Heinrich Heine, or Thomas Mann? But while the cold, crystal-cut German spoke to the thinking mind, Yiddish touched warm emotion, the beating Jewish heart.

The harder they worked to break the ice, the more closed-off and morose she grew. Completely indifferent to wordplay, juicy Jewish humor, winks insinuating a naughty double entendre. In her view, Yiddish was nothing more than a dysfunctional German, the distorted lingo of gypsies. She answered them in the third person, receiving an odd pleasure from shocking them. They restrained their rage, retreating with their tails between their legs.

Later on, they repaid her in their roundabout way. Well-connected friends in the immigration department delayed her citizenship application. Her requests to meet with the head of the department were turned down again and again. At a loss, she contacted the embassy, but even Oscar's attempts to get to the bottom of the delay were for naught.

"I don't understand what's going on," he told her over the phone. "The ambassador's substitute called the legal counsel at the immigration office personally to ask about the delay. The man claims that your file is being reexamined due to security reasons he cannot specify."

The timing was terrible in every way. Himmler's rosy forecasts, which he made to the soldiers of the central army just before Operation Barbarossa—that they would all celebrate Christmas together on the banks of the Volga River—turned out to be misleading. The fate she and William had to look forward to if they were to be exiled to Germany began to seem closer and more palpable than ever. Doubts regarding her security status caused her well-wishers at the Austrian Embassy to ask that she abstain from contacting them directly until further notice. From this point on, she would have to make it on her own.

Gradually, it began to dawn on her that the Jews might be her only allies. From now on, she must treat them graciously and acquiesce to all of their demands. She quickly realized that as a woman, and as a German, she was at the bottom of the food chain. She must therefore officially join the Jewish community and roost beneath its protective wings.

They appointed her to a public service mission. The representatives that came to visit her this time were a famous Hollywood producer of German-Jewish descent and an award-winning director. They offered her a role in an anti-Nazi propaganda film.

Eva smiled vaguely, demurring that she was very flattered, but that unfortunately she had not been blessed with a smidgeon of dramatic talent. Even at school plays, she was always positioned at the rear of the stage.

The bird-faced director paced the room in broken circles, head lowered and hands clasped behind his back. When he heard her make this statement he paused and clapped excitedly. "Bingo!" he cried victoriously. "That's precisely what we're looking for." In a deep baritone entirely at odds with his tiny stature, the director explained that their sole purpose was to show, on live television, that beyond genius minds, the Jewish genome also knew how to produce a true *shikse* that would meet the highest Aryan standards: 178 cm in height, a fit body, sturdy legs, straight flax hair, blue eyes, a slanted nose—and, nevertheless, perfectly Jewish.

They asked her to serve as their secret weapon in their battle against the American isolationist policy led by Charles Lindbergh, America's most decorated pilot and a favorite of Hermann Göring, who had gifted him with a gold medal. Lindbergh, who had objected vehemently to America becoming involved in the war against Nazi Germany, claimed that three interest groups were attempting to urge the United States into a war it had no stake in: The Roosevelt government, the British, and the Jews. Eva's presence would serve as irrefutable proof against Hitler's racial theory. Her punchline would be, "America has a sacred duty to save the world from itself."

The idea that people wanted to use her physical beauty while emphasizing her lowly Semitic origins seemed tantamount to burning a scarlet letter on her forehead. Her eyes downcast, she said, "I take your offer as a great compliment, gentlemen, but sadly I cannot accept."

Otto Schiller, who stood a few paces away, smoking, now crushed his cigarette with a violent twist of the butt and hurried over. "Listen to me carefully, Frau Wittgenstein," he said in German. "We're only talking about a brief cameo. No more than five minutes. All you need to do is speak one line and smile. We'll take care of the rest."

He had a polished Berlin accent. The cultured Jews were the first to flee the country. Otto Schiller was a renowned documentary film producer with a worldwide reputation. He foresaw the future, abandoned a glamorous career in Germany, and arrived in the United States a month before the war began, where he was warmly welcomed into the war propaganda effort.

Eva glared at him defiantly. "And that's going to make a difference?" she spat. "My smile is going to save the world?"

The director came closer. "My dear," he appeased, "a smile like yours is capable of rescuing more people than you can imagine."

"And what exactly must I do?"

"Nothing. Simply nothing. All you have to do is look into the camera, say your one line, and that's it. Cut."

"I can't."

They gave her their business cards and left.

A piece of registered mail that came from the immigration department a week later informed her that they still had not received an original birth certificate or a notarized confirmation of her Jewish ethnicity, and that failure to provide said documents within a month would result in her citizenship application being denied, leading to her immediate deportation.

That was a heavy blow. Germany and its collaborators had advanced quickly but been blocked on most warfronts, leading to a significant retreat in some cases. Amplifying voices among both major Congressional parties were calling on President Roosevelt to forsake his isolationist views and join the allies in their fight to banish the Nazi cancer. Deportation would mean Eva's certain death.

Oscar scolded her for her stubbornness. "You're putting yourself at risk. Worse, you're putting William at risk." Then, his voice hardening, he added, "There's a limit to what we are able to do for you."

He instructed her to start cooperating immediately.

The road to salvation passed through the offices of Dr. Samuel Rosenberg, attorney at law, president of the New York Jewish Community and legal counsel to the Bureau of Population, Refugees, and Migration.

He greeted her with unbidden coldness. When she finished saying her piece, he removed his glasses and fixed her with a withering glare.

"Does Madam understand the meaning of this letter?"

"I suppose so."

"Let me explain it again. In order for you to receive refugee status, you must present documents proving your claims of Jewish faith. This can be a birth certificate, a civil registry file, or an identification card. Do you possess any of these?"

"I do not. We left Germany with twenty-four hours' notice. A week later, the civilian archive in Berlin was bombed and all documents were set on fire."

"In other words, you could be a Jewish refugee, a spy, or a Nazi war criminal in hiding."

Eva flushed. "I'm Jewish," she said hotly. "I'm no Nazi criminal."

Dr. Rosenberg leaned closer. "Do you have any idea, Mrs. von Antrim, how many Nazi war criminals seek shelter in the United States by stealing the identities of their Jewish victims?"

"I'm Jewish."

He nodded dubiously. "I'm afraid I can't help you."

"But I *need* your help."

A mocking smile hovered on the lawyer's thin lips. "That's a surprising thing to hear from the woman who vehemently refused to participate in a film that might have helped her Jewish brethren."

"I explained to them that I was not the right person for the job."

His amused expression evaporated. "Otto Schiller is a top-grade producer," he said firmly. "The best in the business. If he believes you're the best person for the role, then I trust his judgment completely. I think you've made a big mistake, Frau von Antrim."

The fury with which the lawyer pronounced her name gave her chills. Eva apologized for having underestimated the importance of the matter, and declared herself prepared to stand in front of the camera whenever she was needed.

Dr. Rosenberg watched her with contempt as she spoke. When she was finished, a cumbersome silence spread through the room. Then he spoke flatly. "I'm glad we understand each other, Miss. I'm convinced that we will soon learn there has been an unfortunate mistake with regards to your case." He clicked a small switch on his desk and the office door opened. The secretary stood in the doorway. "Please escort Mrs. von Antrim out."

That night, Eva called the director.

William attended a private boys' high school on the Upper East Side. The school was located in an old Edwardian building surrounded by manicured flower beds, green lawns, and ancient chestnut trees. The building used to serve as a theological seminary for prospective Anglican priests. Years later, it was converted into a school for girls of good pedigree that had gone astray. In the early 1940s, the fabulous acoustics in the prayer hall caught the attention of city financiers, who converted the space into a fine concert hall with upholstered velvet seating and a state-of-the-art air conditioning system. Unfortunately, the opening of Lincoln Center heralded the hall's gradual yet consistent decline. Music lovers quickly chose the glitzy, modern concert halls of the new center, and the Upper East Side building stood empty for five years before being put on the market again.

A senior official at City Hall recognized the financial potential of the building, as well as the tasteless American weakness for the slightest whiff of British aroma, and declared the building a historical landmark. After some comprehensive renovations and careful preservation, which revived the building's dulled glamor, it was leased to a not-for-profit association intending to start a Rudolf Steiner school for the children of the nouveau riche who wished to transform their dull-minded offspring into lofty, intellectual connoisseurs.

The deep recession that plagued the United States during the war and the following financial crisis caused a sharp drop in enrollment and transformed the competitive entry terms: The school's gates were now open to anyone who could afford tuition.

The morning session began with a Christian prayer. A large Irish cross adorned with reliefs of saints hung high on the wall. Sounds echoed from the twisting innards of an enormous pipe organ. A handful of Jewish children who had taken their seats in the back rows looked down, careful not to make eye contact with crucified Jesus. Later, when the children of observant Jews from the crowded neighborhoods of Monsey joined the school, their parents demanded that a Jewish prayer be held in a separate room.

The school administration's response was unequivocal: "Out of the question! The foundations of this school were cast to the sounds of Christian prayer. Holy water was sprinkled on the cornerstone."

But when the Jews threatened to remove their children from the school and put an immediate end to their generous donations, the administration changed its tune. And when Jewish children became the majority of the student body, Christian morning prayer was made defunct. The cross was removed shamefully, replaced by a red silk Torah curtain embroidered with the words "How beautiful are your tents, Jacob, your dwelling places, Israel" in gold thread.

Adolescence went by with relative peace. Official word of William's father's death arrived when he was eighteen. His mother, who recognized his grandmother's angular handwriting instantly, slipped on her reading glasses, tore open the gray envelope bearing the family crest, and read the letter out loud, her voice trembling.

In concise statements, his grandmother informed them that his father, who had served on the eastern Russian front, had been killed in the battle of January 10th, 1943, during a heavy northern artillery assault made on Leningrad. The envelope also included his father's last letter, sent from the frontlines. "His final thoughts," his grandmother added toward the end of her missive, "were devoted to the three people dearest to him—his mother, his only son, and his wife."

The second letter arrived four years later, from the office of family notary Charles Atalie, summoning William to Germany at once for the reading of his grandmother's will in her presence.

He received a cold, nearly hostile welcome at the Munich airport. His uncle, Hans, who had been tasked with welcoming him with the warmth deserved by a nephew, waited in the arrivals hall with visible impatience, shaking William's hand as if forced to.

His twin sons, Peter and Heinrich, were gripped with excitement, fidgeting restlessly, but restrained themselves. They seemed to be the products of a strict upbringing. Orphaned of their mother, they were raised under their grandmother's watchful eye.

The ride from the airport was tensely quiet. The uncle answered William's polite chitchat with curt, third-person responses.

His grandmother greeted him in bed. William was appalled by her appearance. Her once tall, firm stature had shriveled, a slight distortion of the upper spine caused her to grow a hump, hunching her body. Her facial features had sharpened, the soft skin gliding off of her once-chiseled face, landing in tender folds over her sunken chest. The tall, large-bodied woman had, over the years, come to resemble a Japanese rice-paper drawing of her old self. Tears streaming down her face, she opened her sagging arms and held him to her emaciated chest, whispering in his ears over and over again, "*Meine kinder, meine kinder*," just as she'd used to when he was a child.

The next morning, her will was read. Joachim, Martha the housekeeper's son, led his grandmother in a wheelchair into her late husband's study. There, with narrowed predator's eyes, she watched the notary's lips as he read out the will, mouthing the words along with him.

The dim room was silent apart from the screeching of the pen moving along bumpy paper and the stamping of documents. Ultimately, William inherited all: the nobility title, the mansion, the Stuttgart factories, the expansive agricultural farms in Harburg, and the ancient vineyards in Mosel-Saar. There were also luxury apartments and office buildings in Munich, rented long-term, a summer castle in Karlsruhe, and a fantastic art collection on loan at the Pinakothek in Munich, on top of an enormous amount of capital wisely invested in Swiss bank government bonds and bearing fine annual yields.

Uncle Hans, in a black suit and a stiff white collar, watched the notary through dull eyes, as if the statements were being spoken in a foreign language. All of a sudden, he turned his head toward William, fixing him with a look of utter contempt. Cousins Peter and Heinrich, curled up in a corner, squeezed into wooden chairs and wore perfectly polished shoes and suits that were too tight for their large bodies. Their canine eyes were lowered submissively. They kept silent, as if afraid to spoil the occasion with their wheezing breaths. Every once in a while, they turned their heads toward William and offered him their innocent, helpless smiles.

William liked them a great deal. There was a kind of thick slowness about their minds and speech. Sometimes it seemed to him that Peter and Heinrich were living in a parallel universe on different, longer, slower timelines. The air in their world must have been a viscous, yellow plasma. They weren't malicious. On the contrary: as children, they had been characterized by a natural, beaming amiability and an unstoppable generosity. They had been obedient.

Even as they failed at school, to their father's great chagrin, their grandmother never gave up on them. One tutor after the next was summoned to the mansion, but all attempts had failed. A world-renowned pedagogical expert who studied them for two whole days at his Berlin practice advised that they be sent to a boys' secondary school in Frankfurt. "They are in dire need of the company of their peers. Sports can also be exceptionally helpful, Madam. I'm talking about challenging sports, competitive sports, the kind that clears minds and encourages success."

They only made it a year at secondary school before dropping out. Conjugating in Latin and memorizing complicated logarithmic equations caused them severe migraines and unbearable chest spasms. The doctor who examined them determined they were perfectly healthy. "Psychosomatic aches and pains," he determined. "They need a looser structure, outdoor spaces, and fresh air."

The bridle was removed and the two began spending most of their time outside. In the daytime, they helped mansion employees with farm work, and in the evenings they went out with young villagers. Being in nature and spending time outside revived their natural, healthy vitality.

The twins were rejected from the military offhand. The official reason was severe cognitive impairment and social incompatibility. This was a hard blow for a family that had spawned many a celebrated military man. A friend of the family who worked as a senior military doctor at the enlistment offices struck the shameful clause from the medical report, and wrote instead that the two were dismissed from military service due to scoliosis and severe flat foot. Their grandmother cried as she read the report. Now William was her only hope.

Squeezed into their seats, Peter and Heinrich watched William in silence while Hans, mad with worry, twisted his face with disgust. His bottom lip trembled, his nose dripped, and he blew it with exaggerated theatricality, promising himself not to give up.

His vapid children, who did not fathom the magnitude of the disaster, accepted the apocalyptic catastrophe spinning over their heads with moronic smiles, drumming their feet impatiently on the wooden floor, breathlessly waiting to burst out of the stuffy office and stride out to the green outdoors. Their tapping drove their father mad.

"Stop that ruckus right this instant!" he screamed, enraged, then turned to his mother, his voice restrained. "You can't do this to me. The inheritance belongs to me and my children." He pushed his children toward her wildly, screaming, "These are your real grandsons! Like it or not, these are true von Antrim boys, every last drop of blood in their veins is purely German." All of a sudden, he turned around and pointed accusingly at William. "Him? Him? He's just a dirty *Jew*."

The French notary Charles Atalie raised a pair of intelligent eyes from his gold-rimmed pince-nez glasses, then lowered them to the will.

William's grandmother's face turned to stone. Her meek voice bubbled toxically. "How dare you speak to me this way! How dare you speak of your dead brother this way! William is my grandson, flesh of my flesh. You have no one in this world beside him."

Later, in her bedroom, she squeezed William's hand. "He didn't mean to hurt you," she said, her voice trembling. "Your uncle Hans has nothing against the Jews. You know, when Rosa Luxemburg and Karl Liebknecht's bodies were pulled out of the lake in Tiergarten, Hans was there to help. He rushed over with a group of boys as soon as he'd heard. He looked up to them, admired their courage. They spent weeks searching. Everybody knew those scoundrels from the Freikorps had shot her in the head not because she was a communist, but because she was Jewish."

William nodded his agreement. He'd read about Rosa Luxemburg and Karl Liebknecht in the newspaper. America was appalled by the murder. But he also knew full-well that many German communists saw their Jewish counterparts as frauds. Secret capitalists. Hans, an enflamed communist in his younger days, was no different. He wasn't afraid to say he suspected them, and consistently avoided their company.

His grandmother did what she could to comfort him. Her efforts were moving. Two days before he returned to America, she called him into her room.

Martha sat her down in an armchair, plumping pillows behind her back. His grandmother's white hair had been braided and wrapped around the top of her head. A soft late September sunset danced among the branches of trees in the garden, and her figure became ephemeral, almost imperceptible. William could sense that she had embarked on her path to those invisible, faraway locales. When he drew nearer to kiss her forehead, she ran a finger against his cheek. Her voice was gruff and meek.

"I want you to promise me something."

"What?"

"I need you to do everything I'm about to ask."

"I'll do my best."

"That's not good enough. I need you to promise."

"I promise."

"I want you to forgive him."

"Who?"

"Hans. He's very ill. This war has ruined him. His nerves are weak, but he's got a kind soul. As a child, he refused to eat meat because he wouldn't harm a living creature." She fell silent for a moment, caught her breath, then continued in an ameliorating tone, "He doesn't hate you. You're his brother's only child. He's simply concerned for his sons' future. You can understand how they worry him, all things considered."

"I forgive him."

The next morning, as he walked Atalie to the train station, William shared the events of the previous night.

"That's what she told you?" the notary asked, slowly sucking on his empty pipe. Then, quickly, he added, "Don't get me wrong, I've known your grandmother for many years. She's a difficult woman, but very humane. Too humane to see reality plainly. Your uncle had been sick long before the war started. Very sick. I remember his rage even from when he was still just a young boy."

"And she never noticed?"

The lawyer shook his head. "No. Lots of people pointed it out to her. First they insinuated. Then they became more explicit. But she wouldn't even hear it. She couldn't accept reality. One can understand her. Who can bear to acknowledge something like that about their own child? Especially when he is such a gentle, intelligent boy, and such a virtuoso with the cello. At first, your grandmother attributed his impulsivity to "artistic sensibilities," as she called it. Later, she claimed it had to do with puberty. At the enlistment office, Hans asked to join the S.S.—an entirely inappropriate choice for a man who would cry at the sight of a wounded animal. He saw himself as a patriot, and believed military service would harden him."

William stopped in his tracks. "He enlisted into the Wehrmacht?"

"Yes. The horrific things he saw and the terrible pressure made his mental health decline even further. Eye witnesses said that during the first *aktion* he took part in, he sent his old cello teacher to be murdered without batting an eye. When he was interrogated in Soviet captivity, he claimed he did it out of humanitarian reasons. In his deposition for military court, he stated, 'The man was old and very ill. He wouldn't have survived a minute in the camps. I did him an act of kindness by sparing him humiliation and hellish agony.' Ultimately, he was acquitted because he was mentally unstable. He spent eight months at a military sanatorium before being discharged." Atalie lit his pipe and sucked on it thoughtfully. "After that, he studied entomology at the University of Hamburg. In spite of his mental state, he was actually not a bad student. His grades were quite good. That's when he became obsessed with collecting butterflies. The walls of his room became covered with wooden plaques skewered with hundreds, maybe thousands of butterflies in stunning colors. A horrifying vision for an alleged animal lover. But even experts attested that his was a remarkable entomological collection."

"Where is the collection now?"

"Nobody knows. He kept changing hiding places. At any rate, only few and privileged people were granted access to his study. Once, when he was in a rare good mood, he invited me to watch how he added new items to his collection. That moment when the pin broke through the insect's keratin coating... that final, desperate flutter of the gorgeous creature's wings... it was appalling. Hans noticed the revulsion on my face and screamed at me to get out. He looked completely crazy then, like a cord in his brain had broken. Your grandmother had no choice but to hospitalize him by force at a psychiatric hospital in Locarno."

"And the collection?"

"No one knows what came of it. The housekeeper claims that the day before Hans was sent to the hospital, he set it on fire in the backyard."

Five months after the reading of the will, William's grandmother died in her sleep. When he arrived for the funeral, he instructed the family bookkeeper to allocate a fair annual allowance to Peter and Heinrich, on the condition that they acquire decent professions.

Indeed, by his next visit, at Christmas, he found the brothers in the mansion offices, sitting side by side behind desks, meticulously copying long lines of numbers.

He could barely recognize them at first. They'd gained weight. Thin, bird-like plumage replaced their previous blond manes. Their faces had wilted, their cheeks covered with tiny hemorrhages from burst capillaries. Copying endless rows of numbers required an immense effort from them. They were sweating, their pressed clothing squeaking against their bodies. When William tried to speak to them, the bookkeeper rushed over, gently took hold of his elbow, and led him out of the room.

"Please refrain, sir," he said apologetically. "They've had a difficult few months. They've become completely unbridled."

"What does that mean?"

The bookkeeper fell silent, his eyes bouncing nervously in their sockets.

"I asked you a question," William growled.

"Violence. Intense violence. Fortunately, the judge took mercy on them, thanks to their deceased grandmother."

"And now?"

"Now they're taking medication that makes them calmer." Noticing William's stunned expression, he added, "even the slightest change to their daily routine could completely derail them."

"They looked so healthy when I'd left. Happy, even."

"The medication is only part of their course of treatment, which also includes psychotherapy. We emphasize a strict routine, nutritious meals, and moderate exercise. That's what they need. Routine affords them a sense of safety and tranquility. They go to bed early now. No more alcohol and gambling. At this rate, we'll be able to find decent wives for them. They have inherited a respectable amount of money from your grandmother, and with the right women by their sides, they might make exceptionally amenable husbands."

When William walked into the room to say goodbye, the two looked up at him with dull, extinguished eyes. They didn't even recognize him.

William encountered his first patient by chance.

It started with a conversation he had with Dr. Juliana Friedman, a psychiatrist at the hospital where he worked. She explained that, because she was fluent in Yiddish and Polish, the municipal department of health had tasked her with preparing a medical report on the Jewish refugees who were quarantined at Ellis Island. William asked to shadow her during one of her weekly visits, and the doctor agreed.

The clinic was actually a refurbished reception hall at the old customs house. The place was dim and derelict, with peeling, dark green walls and crumbling plaster cornices around which enormous spiders had woven floury baroque clusters of dead insects. Narrow windows were open near the ceiling, and a yellow incandescent bulb cast a meager light on the linoleum floor. The air was damp and pungent with Lysol. An old desk and four chairs were the only pieces of furniture in the room.

The first two patients were a couple in their late thirties. The woman walked in first, moving briskly and sitting with her back straight. Her eyes were intense, mad. The man followed her in hesitantly, pausing in the corner of the room.

Juliana waved him over. Then she began to take down their information in her notepad.

The woman turned her head toward William, her eyes piercing through him. Her face was spiritual, beautiful, fragile, sketched with vigorous yet delicate lines. Her skin was pale. Her glistening black hair was pinned to her temples and wrapped in a bun in back. Misery had made deep marks around the corners of her mouth and the sides of her eyes. Her thin lips trembled occasionally. Dark circles around her eyes attested to severe insomnia. The man was curled up beside her, shrunken inside of a black woolen coat that was too big for his stature. His head was lowered, blond tufts of hair peeking from underneath a wide newsboy cap.

All of a sudden, the woman spoke up in Yiddish. "He won't talk to me anymore."

Juliana looked up. "Who won't talk to you?"

The woman turned her eyes to the man. "Him," she said softly.

"Your husband?"

"Yes."

"Is he speaking to other people?"

"He won't speak to anyone."

"When did he stop speaking to you?"

"When they brought him to my camp."

The man raised his head slowly and looked longingly at his wife. His dark eyes burned against his face, pale from the tuberculosis. William looked at him carefully. The man was in agony, eaten up on the inside. An interior burning that would lead him to a premature death. No one would be able to save him.

The two had married in a concentration camp, a quorum of Slabodka Yeshiva students having officiated the ceremony in secret. He was a poor yeshiva boy from a devout Hassidic family, a brilliant, waifish young man who could only ever handle books. She was the daughter of a wealthy, educated fur merchant who had caught the Zionist bug. Their affair caused discontent in both their families.

During the first selection she underwent at Birkenau, the wife was sent to Dr. Mengele's clinic, where she was repeatedly raped. When she became pregnant, an elderly midwife pulled the fetuses from her uterus using contaminated knitting needles that nearly caused her death. Dr. Israel Brauda, who ran the clinic, had saved her life. He injected her with a pricey antibiotic reserved for the S.S., diluted the toxins he was ordered to administer to her, and got her back up on her feet. When his actions were discovered, he was shot on the spot. She swore to herself to name her firstborn after him.

"And what happened to your husband?"

"He volunteered at the Sonderkommando so that he could enter the women's camp and see me. He was supposed to haul the bodies of women who died at the clinic to the crematorium."

"Is that when he stopped speaking to you?"

The woman glanced at her husband lovingly. "No. One time, when he came into the clinic, he witnessed me being raped. It stunned him. He ran out, screaming. I didn't see him again until the camp was liberated. When I did, he was no longer speaking."

Juliana nodded. "Have you tried to have a baby?" she asked tenderly.

The woman's lips trembled again. Her eyes welled up. She wrung her fingers until the knuckles turned white. "He won't touch me, but I want a child. I want to have a child with him," she cried with desperation.

Two hours later, William and Dr. Friedman walked out of the hall and strolled silently toward the dock. It started to rain and the sky darkened. An intense wind stirred waves on the black surface of the water. Screeching seagulls flew chaotically in all directions. Through the screen of fog, the lights of Manhattan twinkled like Atlantis rising from the depths.

Back on the ferry, Juliana leaned back in her seat and closed her eyes.

William was frazzled. "How are you planning on treating them?"

Juliana opened her eyes. "Treating them? In what way?"

"Fertility treatments. I'm talking about a child."

Juliana gave him a long look. "A child?" she mumbled incredulously.

"Yes, a child."

"Having seen these women's mental state, how can you talk to me about children?" She sat up and leaned toward him. "These women are burnt up on the inside," she hissed. "Completely emotionally burnt. What you saw was only a mask. A slough. A shell. Remember the first woman we met? The Polish one? All of her talk of love and feelings are pure mimicry, an imitation of what she remembers from before the war. It was like she was reciting lines from a play. This woman had been violently raped dozens of times by dozens of men. And her man, the mute one, who spent every day hauling the dead bodies of women and little girls just to see her, is a dead man walking. Think about that moment when their eyes met. Imagine what they must have felt at that terrible moment. Who could maintain their sanity after something like that? You tell me."

"They survived."

"Physically, yes."

"You don't have any hope for them?"

"Absolutely not. They are both in very bad emotional states. Irreversible, if you ask me. The man is worse. He is completely dysfunctional. I can't imagine the two of them raising a healthy child."

"Think about her, think about the woman. You're sentencing her to die childless."

"Think about her potential children, William. You're sentencing them to misery."

"With psychological therapy and the help of professionals, she could make a good mother."

Juliana sighed heavily. "Perhaps with another partner, she could make it work. But in her state, she won't be able to handle caring for a child in addition to a dysfunctional husband."

"After everything he went through for her, are you suggesting they divorce?"

Juliana glared at him. "I don't see another way," she said drily. "Do you?"

"I was thinking about in-vitro fertilization, using her husband's sperm."

William decided to publish his article about "America's moral obligation to Jewish refugees from Europe" in *The New York Times* immediately after having read a comprehensive clinical research paper in a famous medical journal, which showed that more than forty percent of extermination camp survivors suffer from endocrinological infertility as a result of prolonged exposure to extreme distress in the camps. In addition, the paper stated, chronic vaginitis and Asherman's syndrome were three times more prevalent in Holocaust survivors than in the average western woman. The problem was that the majority of refugees had yet to receive their American citizenship, and were therefore not entitled to subsidized fertility treatments and sentenced to lives of childless lonesomeness.

William felt it his duty to raise public awareness. Or, as he later stated in court, it was up to him to "generate the enormous rising wave, a wave so powerful that it would shake the seats of those working on Capitol Hill, determining the fates of thousands of Jewish women with the pointing of a finger."

Orvil Salzburg, his childhood friend and the mythological editor of The Times, listened in silence, his stern expression shifting with agreement. "Explosive material," he finally determined. "But we shouldn't discuss this here."

William glanced through the glass walls of the editor's office down at the busy bullpen. "Where do you suggest we meet?"

"The village. Arthur's."

Arthur's Tavern was Orvil's sanctuary, a confessional in the heart of the village's dim burrows of sin. Conspiracies, corruption, blood vengeance, sinful indiscretions, national fates, the destinies of ambitious politicians and power-hungry generals—these were all performed and determined in this small room in the heart of darkness. No bleeding admission or diabolical plan were powerful enough to crack the serene expression on this "priest's" Jewish face as he listened in. He'd seen everything and heard everything.

He bolstered his oracle-like silence with a hearty dinner. As people told him their secrets, he busied himself with the careful chewing of spicy chorizo and potatoes roasted in olive oil, washing them down with fine red wine. The room reserved for him was spacious, its unadorned walls soundproof and coated with embroidered silk wallpaper the color of dark wine. Bronze light fixtures cast shadows on the walls. At the center of the room was a table set for two. One guest at a time.

Orvil would greet them with a small smile. At first, he would invite his counterparts to join him in his feast. Most of them turned the offer down, unable to enjoy even a single bite. They sat there, their stomachs turning and acidic. He would gently nudge them to have a bit of wine, not trying to get them drunk, God forbid, but simply to release their tongues. He wanted them at ease, sober, and sharp like tacks.

"May I offer you some wine?"

"No, thank you."

"How about something stronger?"

"Oh, no. Thanks anyway."

Then, with the ceremonious gestures of a man of the cloth, he wrapped a napkin around his neck, tapped his knife and fork together cheerfully, and began to dig in. Orvil ate in moderation, and the slow, rhythmic chewing of the food put them at ease, like the constant, regular ticking of a grandfather clock. His amiable silence made them feel wanted. If their deprived acts, as cruel as they may be, as twisted as they may be, were not enough to hinder the senior journalist's healthy appetite, that meant they were still worthy of human company, and perhaps even of absolution. The meat, squeezed into the see-through skin membrane of the sausage, was chewed carefully, ground to a pulp. A goblet of fine wine was emptied down to the last drop. Orvil liked to cut to the chase, to insert the needle into the heart of the matter. No need to make excuses. Either way, their fates would be sealed the following day over the newspaper's headlines.

The victims detested him. One hand on their genitals, the other offering him a lude gesture, they accused him of slander, of corrupting supreme American morals, of breaking the right to privacy, and of running his newspaper like a vulgar tabloid. In a well-written editorial piece, Orvil retorted that no value was more precious than the American public's right to know, and that free press was the only robust guard dog of democracy.

He listened intently as William spoke, slicing his sausage into careful coins, their red insides revealed like an open wound. Then he dabbed them with a thin layer of mustard, and chewed with his eyes closed. In between, he nodded with understanding. Finally, with an expression of sublime satisfaction, he wiped his mouth clean, emptied a second glass of wine, hiccupped lightly, opened his paper-thin lids, and revealed his wise owl eyes. "I suggest you rethink this whole thing."

William's voice hardened. "I've thought it through, and I'm determined to publish."

"I'm not sure publishing this would further your interests."

"This isn't about my interests. It's about the interests of the survivors whose time is running out. Their chances of becoming pregnant are dwindling with every passing day."

Orvil stifled a burp with his hand. The decomposing human body still contained the possibility of pleasure, and he wasn't about to spare himself any. "Wouldn't political connections be more efficient?" he asked, feigning innocence. He then added, "Plenty of senior politicians in both parties owe you favors. With the amounts you've been donating, you could receive support from every member of Congress."

"I don't want their help. I need public support. I want every American to feel personally obligated to correct this deplorable moral wrongdoing."

Orvil poured himself some more wine. "You think it's America's duty to correct these European atrocities?" he asked. "Don't you think the United States has more than enough of its own atrocities to worry about?"

"America cannot shirk its responsibility toward European Jews."

Orvil raised a brow. "First and foremost, the United States must deal with its own original sin, committed against the Indians and the Blacks. It is an enormous debt, and us Jews are just going to have to wait our turn."

"That comparison is a dire mistake, Orvil."

"Perhaps. Be that as it may, allow me to tell you that your attitude simply won't work. Not in America, anyway."

"Why not?"

"Let me ask you one simple question. How the hell is this any fault of a homemaker from Cincinnati? How about a good Christian milkman from Wisconsin? Why is he to blame for what the Nazis did to the Jews?"

"Who said anything about blame? I'm talking about a moral, human, religious responsibility—take your pick. I believe that any American who sees himself as a human being must feel an obligation to help these women."

Orvil emptied the bottle. "Absolutely," he said, taking a long sip. "But may I remind you that our Cincinnati homemaker lost a son in Normandy, hundreds of thousands of miles from home. And our milkman from Wisconsin? He was badly injured in Okinawa, leaving him paralyzed from the waist down. A wreck. Now explain to me, what moral obligation are you talking about?"

"Let's start with the puppet masters. You've surely heard Roosevelt's pathetic promise never to send American boys to die in foreign wars, while simultaneously shooting down Edith Rogers's bill that would have allowed 20,000 Jewish children to settle in this country. I'm talking about criminally twiddling his thumbs while intelligence agencies presented the White House with countless classified documents proving that the Nazis had already begun systematically exterminating Jews all over Europe. I'm talking about American fighter jets flying over Auschwitz without bombing it. I'm asking you—why?"

The editor closed his eyes and sighed. Publishing this article would be a terrible mistake. If William wanted to waste his wealth on fertility treatments for Jewish women, that was his funeral. He was rich enough to buy them a second and third child and care for all of their needs. By the same token, he was free to climb to the top of the Empire State Building and shower New Yorkers with a green rain of one-hundred-dollar bills, if that helped him appease his conscience.

Orvil opened his eyes and gave William a languid look. "Are you aware that publishing this may awaken some anti-Semitic demons?"

"That shouldn't be a concern."

"What are you trying to accomplish?"

"I want this issue on the public agenda. I want people discussing it everywhere. At home, at work, at church, at the grocery store. They are going to ask themselves many difficult questions, such as—What did America do to try and save the Jews? More importantly, what is it doing now to help the refugees?"

Orvil shook his head vigorously. "That's a mistake," he said. "You are accusing them. No one likes being accused, William. Especially not Americans, and especially not of crimes they did not commit. Moreover, remember that they suckle solidarity with the weak and less-fortunate along with their mothers' milk. I suggest a change of course: let them feel magnanimous. Appeal to their natural generosity. To their ingrained sense of justice. You'll find them soft and malleable."

"I'm talking about essence," said William, "not tactics."

"The two aren't mutually exclusive. I'm just trying to help you minimize the damage."

"Damage to whom?"

Orvil leaned back, exasperated. "First, to these women you are so worried about. They would be the first to suffer. And don't forget about me—as a stakeholder in the newspaper, this could hurt me as well. I've got sponsors, subscribers, shareholders. I don't live in a vacuum. These people all have firm opinions that don't always align with Jewish interests."

William twisted his face with disappointment. "It's all about money with you," he mocked.

Orvil nodded his agreement. "It's a major concern, but not the only one."

"How does that cliché go? Journalism is the watchdog of democracy?"

A sneaky smile pulled on the corners of Orvil's mouth. "Someone's got to feed that dog."

"I'll bear all financial losses," William declared.

"I doubt we can assess future losses this far in advance, not to mention the fact that this kind of article would necessarily brand the paper with a specific political leaning, while I prefer to maintain political ambivalence as much as possible."

"I'm talking about human rights."

"Many people will see this as strictly political, preferring a specific ethnic minority to others."

"Like who?"

"The Blacks."

"The Blacks?"

"Tens of millions of Black people were tortured and murdered for years, but their troubles never made it to the public sphere—not for long, anyway. That's one thing you can't say about the Jews."

"You've published many articles about Black protests in Pennsylvania, New York, Washington. You published daily pieces about the bus boycott in Montgomery."

"We covered these events objectively. Our pieces offered facts, numbers, exact quotes."

"That's precisely what I'm asking you to do here—cover these women's awful past, the torture, the medical experiments, the disease, the insanity, their mental health, their immense longing for a child."

Orvil gave William a long look. The fervor with which he spoke surprised him. "Okay," he finally said. "We'll publish the articles. But I'm going to edit them."

William objected. The articles would be published word for word, or else he would turn to Orvil's competitors. Worst case scenario, he would pay out of pocket for the articles to be published.

Orvil feigned insult. His heavy head retreated, his pretty eyes glowed under the deep shadow of his wide forehead, and his thick nose hovered over his illuminated face like a decisive exclamation point. "Your articles will be published in *The New York Times*," he announced. "I'm the only one who'll give you this good a platform."

The articles were eventually published on the first page of the paper's festive new year issue. The powerful reactions from readers surprised even the most jaded journalists.

At one o'clock in the afternoon, a group of young people with shaved heads gathered around the Times Building. They were wearing orange Tibetan monastic robes and carrying improvised signs boasting Jewish women's right to procreate. They rang bells, lit incense, and sang with their eyes closed. The evening news reported demonstrations in other cities around the country.

One reaction caught Orvil's attention more than others: Mark Lindbury, the sharp-tongued *Daily Mirror* critic, added a malicious cartoon to an editorial, showing President Truman, with his furious and somewhat bird-like profile, as a female kindergarten teacher. Naked, save for a patriotic stars-and-stripes apron covering her crotch, she whipped the bare bottom of a German toddler with a short mustache, as punishment for beating up her prodigy—a tiny Jewish boy with curly sideburns and an enormous yarmulke. The little Jew, covered with bruises, stands in the corner, tears arching out of his eyes. Above him, floating in a cloud, was the word "*Gevald.*"

Six months after the articles were published, William participated in an international conference on women's health at the Royal College of Physicians in London. By this point, he had published several papers in top medical journals, his research hailed by people in the know as groundbreaking in the area of IVF, positioning him side by side with the world's leading scholars. William had been invited to give the opening statement at the conference's first session.

The auditorium was full of doctors, media people, editors of medical journals, and agents of medical industries. William presented new medication, state-of-the-art devices, and advanced treatment procedures. He then declared his intention of starting a fertility institute in New York. In addition to treating women who could not afford the expensive treatment, the institute would serve as a research center, employing the best people in the field.

To the sound of applause, William walked out of the auditorium and was taken directly to a press conference.

A young health journalist for *The Daily Telegraph* raised his hand and asked what the point was in investing millions of dollars for the procreation of western women, while third-world countries were overpopulated with unwanted babies, some of whom were being tossed in the garbage or flushed down the toilet every single day.

Surprised, William said firmly that, as sorry as he was for the fates of so many children in those countries, this was not a good enough reason to dismiss other women's natural right to bear children.

Some people responded with applause. The journalist raised his hand again. "Do you believe that you, the son of an S.S. Generaloberst who was indicted for racial genocide, have the right to prioritize a certain population over another? Jewish women, for instance?"

The color drained out of William's face. "That's a very serious accusation," he said, his lips trembling. "My father never murdered anyone."

The reporter stood up. "Can you prove this?"

William took a step back.

As if by cue, chaos ensued: several people who had been standing at the back of the room drew closer to the stage, waving swastika flags. They flashed the Nazi salute and yelled, "*Heil* Hitler!"

The host, Doctors Association President Dr. Nicholas Clark, took the microphone and called the ushers to remove the offending parties, who reacted violently. In the tumult, the reporter and his photographer disappeared. Dr. Clark hurried backstage and ordered the building's security guard to capture the runaways before the recordings of the event made it to news agencies.

A brief questioning at *The Daily Telegraph* revealed that the man had been a fraud. His name did not appear in the lists of approved journalists. Dr. Clark said he would make an official statement to the media once things cleared up. In the meantime, the conference would continue as planned, and the doctors were invited to attend the traditional cocktail party after lectures were done.

Upset, William decided to retire to his room.

On his desk, he found a high quality bottle of whiskey and a giant bouquet. The card pinned to the cellophane stated, in German, "In memory of many years of friendship." Having closely examined the card, William called the front desk to find out who had left him these gifts.

The shift manager, an elderly Scotswoman, explained cordially that she had no way of knowing. Packages and flowers were delivered by messenger at the back door. They were handed to the doorman, who gave them to another employee, who placed them in guestrooms.

William was upset. "So you are telling me that objects brought into rooms do not undergo security checks?"

In her most authoritative voice, the woman said, "I apologize for the confusion sir, I must not have been clear. Packages are checked thoroughly. Our orders are to contact the police at the slightest suspicion. My records show that sir's package had been checked, and that the products were delivered in their original packaging."

Encouraged by his silence, the woman made a friendly remark about a potential unresolved romance. "Perhaps a long-lost lover? A rejected paramour? Or maybe just a fan?" Elegant hotels like this one were classic venues for such sweet debauchery. He would be surprised to find how an evolved intellect appeals to women, even young ones. "I, for instance—"

"I'm single," he said flatly. Her insinuations made him sick.

The woman got a hold of herself, and asked, more matter-of-factly, if she could help him with anything else.

"I don't need anything."

"Then I bid sir a good night."

He uncorked the bottle and poured himself a large glass of whiskey. It was very high quality and must have cost a fortune. The liquid slid down his throat, velvety and rich. The effect was immediate. His body gave in without a struggle.

Ninety minutes later, he woke up with an awful headache. The phone on his bedside table had been ringing incessantly and someone was banging on the door. Hair wild, eyes bleary, he opened it.

Dr. Clark was standing in the doorway, wearing a stylish suit. Behind him was a bellboy in uniform. The two looked very concerned. At the sight of William, Dr. Clark breathed a sigh of relief. "I thought something had happened to you," he scolded. He made a face when he got a whiff of the alcohol stench. "Good God, William, look at you."

"I'm exhausted."

"I understand, but you must attend the cocktail party tonight. Eight o'clock, sharp. The reception starts at half past seven. There are many important people who are expecting you there."

William collapsed back into bed. At seven o'clock, the alarm went off. Still sleepy, he called the front desk and asked that Dr. Clark be informed that he would not be attending the cocktail party due to a headache.

Two minutes later, the phone rang. Dr. Clark was on the line. "I understand," he said tenderly. "The last thing I'd want is to disturb you, especially after this day's troubling events. But, luckily, many investors have shown interest in your new project, and they can't wait to meet you."

"I really can't."

"Missing the party would only validate that scoundrel's lies."

William wished to bark at the British doctor's kind voice that perhaps that scoundrel *had* been right. His father's heroic death, as depicted in his grandmother's letter, had raised many doubts in his mind. The military death certificate was sloppily filled out. The cause of death was crossed out and the place of death had been altered. His ranks, pipe, and watch were missing from his personal effects, which had been delivered in a wooden crate, along with the coffin. When he'd asked Atalie, the notary, if he was in possession of any official Wehrmacht documents that supported his grandmother's version of the events, the man replied that he was not.

"I'm just exhausted," William said over the phone.

But Dr. Clark was determined. "You've certainly had a hard day. What you need is a refreshing cold shower and a small, stiff drink to loosen you up. We'll leave the rest to your personal charm."

"I'll come down, but only for an hour."

"Wonderful. An hour is more than enough."

During the first few minutes, Dr. Clark introduced him to some famous American doctors and others he had defined as the most important players in the European medical industry. Then he took a champagne flute from one of the servers, handed it to William, and disappeared.

The atmosphere was jovial. A string quartet played waltzes, women in gowns and men in frocks swayed along the dancefloor. William was chatting with a group of doctors from Milan when suddenly he spotted a middle-aged man standing by the band, watching him from afar. Whenever their eyes met, the man raised his wine glass in greeting, and smiled. His smile was a mocking spasm. The man's wide face was divided by a horizontal scar. The lips stretched upward in a smile, but the rest of the face remained expressionless.

William glanced briefly at the tag on the man's lapel, and cried cheerfully, "German?!"

"Bingo." That malicious smile appeared again, and the man raised his glass once more. "*Prost.*" The man took a tiny sip through pursed lips.

William raised his tumbler of whiskey and gulped it down.

"Seems you've had a difficult day."

"Yes," William mumbled, surprised.

The man nodded. "That reporter was right, wasn't he?" Then, at the sight of William's enraged face, he said, "I only meant to say that it's awful what's happening to millions of children in India, China, Africa. Dr. von Antrim, don't you think—"

"Do I know you?" William asked, cutting him off.

"We've never met in person, but I've had the pleasure of personally knowing your father."

William looked at him bleakly. "What does that mean?"

"Well, I knew him well enough, to be exact. No one could say they knew him personally. Your father was an introverted man."

William took hold of the man's arm. "Tell me about him. I've got so many questions."

That evil, distorted smile appeared again. The man gestured toward the busy ballroom. "This isn't the place to reminisce."

"Where, then? When? You tell me."

The man suggested they meet the following day, right after the morning session's opening lecture. "I'll wait for you outside the auditorium." He placed his full glass on a nearby table and left.

The next day, they walked toward Mayfair, where the man confidently led William through a maze of narrow streets to a small café on Gilbert Street. The place was empty. The man, who was a gynecologist, suggested they have a light breakfast.

William refused politely. "Thank you, but a coffee will do just fine."

The man sipped on his coffee slowly, not speaking a single word, looking over William closely, the ironic smile never leaving his face. Occasionally he stirred the beverage, a quick and involuntary tremble passing through his wide face, wiping his smile away.

A nervous tic? Nerve damage? Facialis? The man's blue eyes were unusually cold. The scar stretched from the right side of the upper lip to his left earlobe. Most likely a well-healed injury from a sharp object. There was also evidence of a later attempt at blurring it through plastic surgery, but the red scar tissue that remained never smoothed itself out. The scar was what made every smile into a sarcastic gesture of derision.

The man's fingers were stubby, thick; the nails trimmed to the quick. If he was indeed a doctor, he was most likely a surgeon, or a rather successful orthopedist. The expensive suit, the Italian leather shoes, and the luxury watch all attested to fantastic socio-economic status.

When he finished his coffee, the man wiped his lips carefully, smiled, and introduced himself as a gynecological specialist from Mecklenburg. "Dr. Karl Gunter, at your service." Then he embarked on a series of questions. "Von Antrim, correct? Dr. William von Antrim?"

"That's me."

"Wittgenstein?"

"On my mother's side."

"Your father was a Generaloberst?"

"I believe so."

"You believe so?" the man's voice was full of reproach.

"I was too young to understand military ranks when we parted ways. I only found out later."

"Do you know what came of him?"

"My grandmother told me he was killed on the eastern front."

"At the siege of Leningrad."

"You were there?"

"I was."

"So you knew him."

"I knew each and every one of our German heroes."

This was the first time he'd heard the word "heroes" spoken about Nazi soldiers. In the America of his childhood, the word "Nazi" had become an abstract term, lending itself to the most satanical descriptions one could conjure up. "Were you with him when he died?"

The gynecologist shifted his eyes out to the garden. A little squirrel was scuffling with a pinecone on the lawn. He watched, mesmerized. Then, suddenly, he spoke. "Do you have any idea how many squirrels we had to hunt during the war just to stay alive? Toward the end, the men even broke down and ate our search dogs."

William made a face.

The man chuckled, the scar splitting his face in two. "So what do you know about the circumstances of your father's death?"

William listed the facts as he remembered them from his grandmother's letter: his father had served as an operations officer for the Russian eastern front. He was injured by shrapnel from a shell that invaded his legs during one of the allies' aerial attacks. Nothing that couldn't be treated properly, even in field conditions. With the help of some basic first aid such as sterile bandages, disinfectant, and antibiotics, he could have easily survived. But due to severe weather conditions, nonstop bombing by the Red Army, and snowfall blocking all escape routes, medical aid was late to arrive, and he lay there in agony. "When he felt there was no more hope left, he begged the other men to put an end to his suffering, finishing him in a manner worthy of a German soldier—a bullet to the head. But no one dared kill a Generaloberst. He ended up dying of sepsis."

"That's what they told you?"

"Is it true?"

"Your father was a hero, period. What difference does it make how he died?"

"I find it hard to believe," William barked, "that you dragged me out here just to tell me it doesn't matter how he died."

"You'll find out everything eventually," the gynecologist said softly. "But right now, we must discuss something far more important."

"What's that?"

"We've been watching you for a long time."

"Watching?"

"Yes."

"To what end?"

"To protect you."

"I'm an obstetrician. What danger could I possibly be in?"

"You're the only son of one of our party leaders."

"And who would want to hurt me?"

The gynecologist leaned back. "Who wouldn't?" he guffawed, his expression forgiving. "Let's start with a few Jews looking for revenge. There are also some rumors about some fine Germans who don't take kindly to your little Jewish project. For now, we're making every effort to stop them."

"We?"

"We."

William said nothing for a long time. Finally, he asked, "Who's we?"

The gynecologist explained quietly that he was part of a group of Germans who made it their mission to bolster national spirit in the low period that followed the war. Their activity revolved mainly around assisting the younger generation. They saw William as his father's heir, and were so surprised by his fertility project for Jewish women that they felt compelled to come forward. The humiliating interaction with the reporter the previous night was their way of giving him a subtle hint.

William turned pale. "Hold on, let me get this straight... that journalist... his questions... that was all staged?"

The gynecologist looked away, quickly moving his eyes over the other people in the room. "Your coffee is getting cold," he said plainly.

"Forget the damn coffee. I asked you a question."

"I'd say it's our polite way of making a point."

"What are you going to do if I don't play along?" he glowered. "Kill me? Ruin my career?"

"On the contrary. We're here to protect you."

William laughed nervously. "Protect me? Good God. By sending a reporter to turn me into a walking target?"

"If you honor our request, no harm will come to you."

"Is that a threat?"

"It's a plea."

William downed the rest of his coffee. "So how long have you been... watching me?" he asked, his tone defiant.

The gynecologist crushed his napkin into a ball. "Since you and your mother left Germany."

William shook his head. "That's insane."

"It's our obligation to German heroes who fought on the frontlines and sacrificed their lives. You were carefully supervised at every given moment."

Inexplicable events now started to make sense. That protective shield he sensed around himself was not a figment of his imagination. For instance, his teachers' respectful, sometimes distant attitude toward him. The teasing from his high school classmates, which stopped abruptly. Someone had been pulling strings in the dark.

And there was Oscar, that faceless oracle from the Austrian embassy, who was always ready to help, but vehemently refused to meet his mother in person.

The gynecologist began to reminisce about William's past. He named places, dates, people.

William stared at him, terrified. "Who are you?" he murmured.

The scar stretched into a smile.

"Who are your people?"

"Patriots."

"Nazis!"

The man's face darkened. "German patriots," he said

sternly. "Your father was a Generaloberst in the S.S., and served as a camp commander in Trawniki. I was his personal doctor. After he was executed by the Russians, I was the one who signed the death certificate."

William's eyes widened. "My father was in the S.S.?"

"He volunteered."

"So he didn't die of sepsis?"

The man's thin lips formed a vengeful smile. "He was executed."

"By firing squad?"

"Why should that matter?"

William stood up and leaned close to the gynecologist's face. The red, beating scar filled his field of vision. "It matters to me," he whispered hatefully. "I want to know how that filthy murderer died."

The man said nothing for a long time. Finally, he spoke. "They hanged him. They hanged him until his soul left his body."

William jumped back, pushing his chair. The coffee cup rolled off the table and crashed to the floor. His face distorted with loathing, he walked out into the garden, where he threw up among the chrysanthemums and the azaleas.

The server that had been standing behind the counter came over to the table. "Is everything all right?" she ventured.

The gynecologist smiled. "Fine," he said. "Our young friend is having some stomach trouble. A cup of herbal tea would do him wonders. And while you're at it, I would love some more coffee."

The girl glanced at William with concern and went to

the kitchen. She returned a few moments later, tray in hand. "He looks terrible," she said. "Should I take the tea out to the garden?"

"No need. He'll recover in a few minutes and come back inside." He sipped his coffee, occasionally glancing at William, who was sitting on a bench in the garden, head in his hands. The first symptoms of shock had appeared, as expected. Meek wives and elderly mothers with unsteady nerves typically reacted with hysterical crying, vomiting, uncontrollable trembling. In extreme cases, they fainted. In young people, reactions ranged from a few shed tears to complete indifference. These strengthened the man's assumption that embedding collective blame in the malleable consciousness of the younger generation was disastrous. Even worse was the pacifist upbringing that was meant to shape the image of the new German generation as following a liberal, humane worldview. This ended up causing severe psychological damage. The gynecologist's conclusion was that oppressing the nationalist sentiment that naturally thrived in the hearts of the younger generation would lead to the weakening of the entire race. Instead of powerful, goal-oriented men, the streets would be filled with confused, hollow-eyed youth. Their self-loathing explained the sweeping wave of suicide that had immediately followed the war, one matched only by the one that followed the needless publication of Goethe's *The Sorrows of Young Werther.*

Unexpectedly, it turned out that denying one's Nazi past was more common among the families of soldiers of low socio-economic status. These less-fortunate families tended to hide their Nazi pasts any way they could. They changed their last names and their places of residence. Bold Gestapo fighters removed tattoos through painful surgery. With a single breath, top S.S. officers became faceless pencil pushers who had spent the war filing endless mountains of paperwork.

Noble families, on the other hand, the ones whose veins flowed with pure German blood, carried their Nazi pasts with pride. These families were cut from hearty, sturdy, Teutonic cloth. The gynecologist called them, "the bone marrow of the German spirit." These people admitted their actions without obfuscation, denying the guilt they entailed while defending the German national spirit as if their lives depended on it. As far as they were concerned, William had a great future as a leader of their party. But for that to happen, he had to get a hold of himself and fast.

The gynecologist stepped out into the garden and took a seat beside William. He stretched out his legs and closed his eyes. The wind picked up and the elm trees screeched heavily. In the distance, the bells of Saint Paul's Church echoed. A flock of crows rose in a single cluster from the tree tops, scattering through the air in heartrending screams. Servers hurried outside to clear the garden tables and the gynecologist suggested to William that they go back inside.

William refused.

The two were silent for long moments. Finally, the gynecologist spoke. "By the way, your project isn't all that original."

"Being original was never my goal."

"Have you heard of Himmler's Lebensborn Program?"

William didn't answer.

"One of our finest projects," the gynecologist continued. "Thousands of German and Scandinavian girls were impregnated by senior Irish officers. In four years, Himmler managed to double the number of beds. 16,000 pure-race children were born in our two centers in Germany and Norway."

"That's sick."

The man's lips twisted. "Sick? I don't see much of a difference between the two projects, save for the fact that yours hinders German interests."

"Does the fact that I'm half-Jewish not hinder your German interests?"

The gynecologist stood up tall. "Here are a few facts for you," he said. "Let's start with the fact that your mother is a Protestant, just like the rest of your family. Generations of Protestants. Whoever gave the Gestapo that false information was only trying to get your father removed from office."

"Then why didn't you bring us back to Germany when you discovered my mother was Aryan?"

"You were someplace safe. Germany was hell on earth back then. The world tends to forget that close to two million German civilians were killed during the war."

"And later?"

"Your grandmother insisted you stay in America. She said your uncle Hans would not be able to bear your presence."

"So she knew I wasn't Jewish all along."

The man smiled. "You didn't really think your grandmother would have let a *mischling* become the heir of the von Antrim fortune, did you?"

William laughed wildly.

The gynecologist narrowed his eyes. "What's so funny?"

"This madness. My mother lights the Shabbat candles every week. She attends synagogue. She recently started taking Hebrew lessons. She says she'd never felt this connected to God. She says she wants to remarry, but only if she can find a Jewish husband. She recently joined the National Council of Jewish Women. She gives thousands of dollars to the community every year."

The gynecologist's face flushed. "Have all the fun you want with your father's German fortune," he fumed. "Play the part of the conscientious American philanthropist until you're completely broke. But know this—you were born German, to a true German father. You can never escape this fact. I'm only here to warn you not to stand in our way." Then he turned and left.

William turned his head back and closed his eyes. When the rain began to fall, he walked back inside. On the table, he spotted a manila envelope bearing his name in print. He tore it open and pulled out an old black-and-white photograph. He stared at it for a long moment, his brain refusing to process the image. His chest caved in, as if someone had wrapped iron fingers around his neck and squeezed, slowly draining his lungs of air. He shut his eyes tightly, wishing to stop the awful images with the power of his lids. When he opened his eyes again, he saw the server watching him with concern.

"Sir, are you feeling all right?"

"Just a little lightheaded," he mumbled. "Please call me a taxi." When he asked for the check, she signaled to him with a wave of her hand that it had already been taken care of. Her grateful smile told him that the tip had been exceptionally generous.

Back at the hotel, he asked the elderly Scottish clerk—who now treated him coldly—for information about the German gynecologist. Having perused her records for a long time, she stated drily that her lists contained no mention of a German gynecologist with a face scar.

"For your information," she added, "many doctors are only auditing the conference, which means they have enrolled without specifying their field of expertise. Most of them are staying at other hotels in the area."

The image of his father from the photograph appeared in full detail in his dreams. The black uniform, the twinkling ranks, the taut stance. In the picture, he looked smug, arrogant, evil. At his side, the gynecologist jutted out his chin in a mocking smile, as if predicting the future, his face still smooth and unblemished.

To their left, in the background, horror ensued. Six tiny figures in striped outfits were hanging from the gallows, frozen in acute angles, their heads collapsed over their broken necks like question marks that would never be answered.

Erica Elizabetha Eisner's first lawsuit against Dr. William Ludwig von Antrim was submitted to the New York Federal Court on June 10th, 1960. Every attempt made by his attorney, Blumenthal, to reject the lawsuit, had been denied.

In his ruling, the honorable John Paul Roberts wrote that past experience teaches us that this sort of charge would necessarily entail further lawsuits made against the defendant, and therefore it would be prudent to wait in order to allow additional patients to file their own lawsuits against Dr. von Antrim, at which time the court would discuss them as a class action.

William asked Blumenthal to offer the plaintiff generous compensation in exchange for withdrawing the suit and extending an apology. "Dr. von Antrim holds no grudges," Blumenthal wrote to the woman's lawyer. "Any apology would be accepted."

Erica rejected the offer with contempt. In a strongly worded letter, her lawyer, Dr. Daniel Goldstone, wrote that his client was appalled by any offer of a plea bargain, and that she was suing the defendant in the name of millions of Jewish women.

More lawsuits began piling up on Blumenthal's desk. He couldn't sleep. He couldn't eat. His wife, who was used to his outgoing, extroverted personality, hardly recognized him now. The overweight, overconfident student who had been hailed as a wunderkind had become, in the course of two months, a pale shadow of his former self. At some point, she feared he may have contracted a malignant disease. He'd dropped forty-five pounds. Distress seemed to have emptied him out from the inside. His shoulders slumped, his chest and potbelly shriveled, his satiated face wilted, and his entire being wizened into an enormous dried fig.

His psychological symptoms were even worse. Blumenthal, who had abandoned the yeshiva in favor of Columbia Law School as a young man—to his devout father's chagrin—now began to pray and use *tefillin* again. One morning, he headed out to the courthouse in a black silk yarmulke and woolen fringes dangling over his pants. His terrified wife saw these as clear signs of an approaching nervous breakdown. She begged him to see a doctor.

"If things keep going this way, it's only a matter of time before involuntary confinement," she told him.

William demanded an explanation.

Blumenthal chose his words carefully. "We've done everything we can," he murmured, "but things have gotten out of hand."

"How many lawsuits are there now?"

"We don't have a final number yet. We receive new ones almost every day."

"How many? I want numbers."

"At the moment, there are sixty-seven lawsuits, and they are adding up at an average rate of four per week. The media circus around Erica's case sped things up, although just recently there's been a noticeable decline—"

"Dear God!"

Blumenthal felt his stomach sink. His bladder was about to explode. He fidgeted, desperately needing to use the bathroom. But William's piercing gaze paralyzed him. He had warned William that offering monetary compensation was tantamount to an admission of guilt, but William had insisted.

The volume of media attention was unprecedented. Losing the suit would cause immense damage to his reputation as a top attorney. Sometimes, he thought this was punishment from God for having deserted his promising future as a brilliant yeshiva boy and gone on to graduate from Columbia cum laude. He had interned at one of the biggest law firms in the city, and within ten years was considered one of the ten best criminal lawyers in the country.

"Revenge," said William. "She wants revenge for what the Nazis did to her. Instead, she'll only end up hurting so many other refugees who can't afford to have a child."

Softly, Blumenthal said, "She claims it isn't about revenge. She says her purpose is to spare other women from similar suffering."

"Suffering? My God, what suffering is she talking about? She was so sick when she came to see me. Nearly barren. Her botched abortion attempts after becoming impregnated through rape had scarred her uterus almost irrevocably. Her husband was nearly a lost cause. She left happy and content, with a child of her own. What suffering could she possibly be talking about?"

"She wrote that it was unimaginable for Jewish women who had been spared from the Nazi inferno to be fertilized by Nazi semen."

William flushed. "I'm not a Nazi," he mumbled, stunned.

"But you are German, and to her the two are the same. In her deposition, she wrote that, had she known the source of the donation, she would have chosen to die childless."

"That's a lie! She asked for the donation to come from a white man. She asked that he be non-Jewish, so that the child wouldn't be a bastard. Beyond that, she explicitly said there were no other demands."

"We have to file a countersuit," said Blumenthal. "She's viewing your offer of compensation as an admission of guilt."

"What do you mean?"

"We must file a defamation suit. A lawsuit demanding a few million dollars will scare her off. She'll withdraw her own lawsuit, and other patients will be deterred, too. It isn't too late. We'll do a little research. There are some pretty nasty rumors about her."

William shook his head. "We're not filing a lawsuit, period," he whispered. "We'll reach a fair deal and be done with it."

"She isn't interested in money. Losing would mean financial catastrophe."

"Find a way out."

"I want her to get a paternity test."

"I'm the father of the baby."
"Are you certain?"
"Beyond a shadow of a doubt."
"We should still have her do it."
"I'm telling you, that child is mine."

Prosecutor Daniel Goldstone had to give William credit when he discovered he'd retained the services of Blumenthal. Choosing a top-notch defense lawyer who was also an orthodox Jew was a brilliant tactic. The New York State bar was swamped with highly ambitious lawyers who were willing to represent Dr. von Antrim, free of charge. The court case received immense global attention. Local and foreign television stations covered the trial every day, broadcasting it at the start of the evening news. Blumenthal was the absolute best. His only point of weakness was his over-the-top theatricality.

Although his wife, Ida, was a fairly famous actress, Dr. Goldstone abhorred the theatre. He despised the stuffy air, the claustrophobic darkness, the physical proximity to strangers. Most of all, he hated the toxic grip of Beckett, the avant-garde alienation of Brecht, the threatening absurdism of Harold Pinter. In his opinion, the one true stage, where witty dialogue lived alongside bloodletting, was the courtroom, period.

He often told Ida, "Come to court with me, and you'll witness the greatest plays you've ever seen. You won't find better actors anywhere on Broadway."

"Thank you for the invitation, darling," Ida replied sweetly. "I've already played the main character in the greatest tragedy of my own life. Now is the time for comedy."

Ida had studied acting at one of the top drama schools in Krakow, but her studies were cut short when the war broke out. In America, she attended nursing school and worked at the Mount Sinai labor and delivery unit almost until the day she died. Even in the early, bad years, when they were starving young people, she insisted on paying for a theatre membership. When their children were grown up, she joined the Yiddish Theatre on the Lower East Side. Acting school in Europe, her natural Jewish mannerisms, and her fluency in juicy Yiddish all made her a natural born star. She handily secured all the major roles, and her rich repertoire included the role of Leah in *The Dybbuk*, Golda in *Fiddler on the Roof*, and Mirale in *Mirale Efrat*.

When Goldstone wanted to make her happy, he joined her at Broadway premiers. When he did, Ida insisted on formal wear: black three-piece suits, shiny black shoes, and a white bowtie for him, bold evening gowns, wild hats, and high-heeled stiletto shoes for herself. She wore excessive makeup, her thin lips thickened with pencil and painted a dark purple. Her green eyes stood out against the backdrop of dark eyeshadow, her eyebrows violently tweezed and redrawn, her cheeks powdered marble-white.

After joining her for three premiers, he'd had enough. The stench of alcohol and cigarette smoke, jazz music playing at mad decibels—it was all more than he could take. He much preferred the tattered leather chair in his study, the green-hued light of the reading lamp, and the dank odor of old books.

She often forced him to admit that he actually had a decent time at the theatre. He found the Greek classics, for instance, more or less bearable. He liked modernized versions of Shakespeare, Marlowe, and Molière. He hailed Franco Zeffirelli's adaptation of *Romeo and Juliet* as brilliant, refreshing, and thought provoking.

But avant-garde theatre was nerve-racking for him. The plots were far-fetched, the characters transparent and plagued with empty mannerisms. The dialogues were unbelievable, peppered with nonstop vulgarity. The crass nudity and the long pauses were pregnant with meaning he could not interpret.

After watching one of these plays, as they walked back toward the car, he told her that it had made him feel desperate, but mostly revolted. He couldn't imagine what deep existential significance could possibly be contained in the cellulite-laden buttocks of the main actress, who had spent the play lying on a bed in the center of a barren stage, fully naked, whining her lines. Or, for that matter, in the shriveled genitals of her aging husband, who circled her like a somnambulant, shaking his fists at the sky and yelling at God in pristine Goethe German, "If you're as all-powerful as you claim to be, then get down here and fight me like a man!"

Ida replied that the crumbling naked body articulated a wordless yet loud, unignorable statement.

Once, having viewed an exhibition of rare photographs taken by ally soldiers at Birkenau and Theresienstadt, she came home in a state of agitation. She said that, as she'd stood facing one of the photographs, she finally fathomed the mute power of the naked human body, just at the place where words had lost all meaning.

The image that had caught her attention was an enormous black-and-white print: a skeletal young woman in defiant frontal nudity, shaved head, and sunken eyes gazing hollowly at the lens. The woman stood at an angle, her white skin wizened and taut over the brittle bones. Her head was titled to the side, as if to glance sidelong at the viewer. She seemed to be in a far-gone, spiritual state. Beside her, at an arrogant *contrapunct*, was a short German officer, fattened like a pig, his face overstuffed, his beady eyes reminiscent of a mouse and pushing outward with a bold, devilish willpower. The man was dressed in an S.S. uniform so tight it seemed about to burst at the seams, tall riding books, and a shiny cap with a skull insignia at its center.

Ida had stared at the image for a long time. There was something riveting and terrifying about it. Oddly, she found that the wonderful aesthetics had only highlighted its monstrous diabolical quality.

Goldstone listened to her, startled. The newspaper slipped out of his hands. Trapped in the dangerous honey of her eyes, his mouth fell open. To him, what she was saying was menacing and appalling. The piles of old shoes and false teeth that belonged to the victims of Auschwitz may have been viewed by avant-garde artists as glorious, groundbreaking works of art, just as famous American art critics examined an enormous colorful installation of cars that had been totaled in lethal wrecks and compressed into a lump of metal at the Metropolitan Museum of Art. It wasn't out of the realm of imagination to assume that future art textbooks would mention the Jewish people as having foretold the beginning of the postmodern art era with their own bodies.

When she died of cancer, he didn't cry.

In her will, Ida only included one request: to have her sons say a prayer for her soul every Saturday, at synagogue. She wrote that she forgave God completely—for the camps, the incinerators, the electric fences, the smoking chimneys. She forgave him for the dead relatives, for the pain and suffering of her disease—thanks to the wonderful family he'd given her. "Thanks to you," she wrote, addressing her husband, "I can die happy."

It brought to mind an old argument they'd had about the Jewish upbringing she wished to give to their children. Goldstone had objected, and the exchange soon turned nasty. Ida was close to tears when she spat at him that only an angry, bitter Jew like him was willing to build the Tower of Babel brick by brick with his own hands, all for the purpose of climbing to the top and challenging God to a fight.

Furious, Goldstone got up and walked out onto the balcony.

Ida followed suit. "You're going to bring tragedy on all of us," she cried, voice trembling.

"That's the fear talking!" he screamed. "You never truly forgave him. You hate him. God, how you hate him. How could you ever forgive him for something like that? Just admit it already—you hate God. Get it off your chest. You have no idea how much better you'll feel."

"I don't hate him, I'm angry with him."

"You're lying to yourself."

After that, they sat in silence for a long time while their three sons played by the pool. Still upset, Goldstone put down his evening paper and began to circle the porch, sucking fervently on his pipe. All of a sudden, he paused in front of her. "You're worried about the children, aren't you?"

Ida took a deep breath and closed her eyes. "Stop talking like that," she whispered, her voice trembling. "I beg of you, stop it."

But Goldstone wouldn't. "You're afraid something terrible is going to happen to them." He leaned closer. "Answer me."

Ida nodded.

"Are you worried someone might build extermination camps in New York?" he hissed. "Are you afraid of seeing crematorium chimneys on Broadway? Or concentration camps in Brooklyn?"

Ida covered her ears with her hands, her body rocking back and forth as if in prayer. "I'm begging you, stop it. Please, stop it."

Goldstone took hold of her shoulders and shook her, hard. His eyes shone madly. "What have we done to deserve this?" he yelled. "Answer me! What did the little children in Europe do? What sin had the newborn babies committed? What?"

"I don't know," she sobbed. "I'm scared."

All of a sudden, he kneeled and cupped her face. "Stop being afraid," he cried. "Stop being afraid."

She burst into tears. "But I am. I'm so afraid." Tears drenched her face.

Goldstone held her close. "Enough," he said. "We don't need to be afraid anymore."

She sunk her nails into his arm. "You must pray. Ask forgiveness."

He guffawed, his laugh like a spasm. "What exactly should I apologize for?" he hissed. "What should we be begging forgiveness for? The Inquisition? The blood libels? The pogroms in Kishinev? Perhaps for Auschwitz? Perhaps for 3,000 years of blind loyalty? What?"

Ida pointed a trembling finger at the children, squealing and frolicking in the yard. "Look at them," she warned. "Look at them carefully before you open your big mouth. Look at me, look at this house, and stop being so ungrateful. Don't you see what God has given you? What he's given us?"

The ball landed on the porch. The children chorused a plea for their parents to throw it back.

Goldstone tossed the ball over, then sat down in a wicker chair, lit his pipe, and took a deep puff. After keeping his eyes on the children scampering on the edge of the pool for a long time, he said there wasn't a single moment in his life when he didn't think of everything God had taken away from him.

Ida was thirty-two when they got married. Goldstone, six years younger, was an industrious lawyer who was forging a persistent path toward the position of attorney general. Their efforts at conceiving failed again and again. At some point, she met with a famous expert, who sent them on an extensive series of tests. The results were satisfactory. Thrilled, she wished to call her husband and share the good news. The doctor objected.

"I would advise against that."

"Why?"

"Your good news could be very bad news for him."

"Shouldn't he be glad that the test results were good?"

"Unfortunately, his sperm count shows a miniscule percentage of properly functional cells. Medically speaking, your husband is barren. Chances of successful sperm washing are meager. Your only options are sperm donation or adoption."

Ida's lips trembled. "My husband must have his own child. He must. He's the only survivor of his family. He'll never agree to use another man's sperm. Never."

The doctor nodded sadly. "Many women choose not to tell their husbands about the donation. In many cases, ignorance saved their marriages."

"Are you telling me to lie to him?"

"I'm not telling you anything."

I**ntent** on fulfilling their deceased mother's final wish, the children spoke the *Kaddish* prayer with broken voices. Goldstone stood beside them, eyes dry. Furious, prepared to defy, to shake his fists. The sight of her body wrapped with a *tallit* on the edge of an open grave made him hold his tongue. When the people from the burial society leaned in and softly offered him a tranquilizer, he barked at them to leave him alone.

Then, in a whisper, he rolled the words through his mouth in an ancient Lubavitcher tune. "*Yisgadal v'yiskaddash shemey raba.*" The final words of the Kaddish were swallowed by a restrained sob. When her body was lowered into the ground, he collapsed, screaming at the top of his lungs, "*Oh, mein libe, mein froi, oh mein got, oy vey, ribono shel oilom was walt ich tan en ir!*"

His children took hold of his arms and brought him back up to his feet, supporting him from all sides. It was no surprise that they couldn't understand the meaning of their father's words. When he came to America, Goldstone erased from his mind not only the Yiddish language, but also the flavors, the scents, the prayers, and tender words such as *patter, mutter, zeide, bubbe, zeis,* and *goylem*.

"Yiddish is Europe, and European air is toxic," he'd told Ida. "It'll poison our children."

Ida looked at him as if he were mad. "You want us to raise them without an identity, Torn," she said bitterly. "Children must know their roots. You can't deny them that."

Flatly, Goldstone replied that their roots were buried in Europe, deep in the dirt, rotting. Here in America, they would grow new, healthier ones.

Ida would sing to the children Yiddish songs, light the Shabbat candles. She baked fragrant challahs and cooked stuffed fish, kugel, and *tzimmes*. As they ate, she told them the tales of Hershel of Ostropol, of Rabbi Levi Yitzchak of Berditchev. The children ate it all up while Goldstone stood nearby, frying himself a steak, chuckling.

"You need good stories when you eat Jewish food," she explained.

When she asked him to say the *Kiddush*, or at the very least a blessing for the challahs, he refused vehemently. "Try again in the next generation," he mocked. "Maybe the grandchildren. Or, better yet, the great-grandchildren. And even then, in small doses, so that they may develop antibodies against Jewish neurosis."

Ida wrapped a white silk scarf around her head and poured wine into the goblet. From his study on the second floor, he heard her saying the Kiddush in her deep, operatic voice, while the children's laughter rang out.

To toughen them up, Goldstone hung a punching bag on the back porch. He spent weekends huffing with them around the abandoned racetrack outside of the Catholic school near their home. They went on long bike rides, played baseball, and wrestled mercilessly. His blows were painful and precise, and he allowed them to hit him back, hard. When they stumbled and fell, he scolded them to get back up again.

To make sure they didn't grow up to be complete idiots, he also pushed them to excel in school. After all, they were the grandchildren of a Torah scholar. On Saturdays, he read fine literature to them, carefully choosing the best, most American authors: hard, bitter. Hemingway, naturally, but also Mark Twain, Edgar Allan Poe, and John Steinbeck, along with a few choice plays by Shakespeare and George Bernard Shaw.

On Sundays, Ida sent them to Hebrew school, where she demanded that the teachers use an Israeli accent. Her efforts bore fruit: only a few years later, after receiving a full scholarship to attend Columbia Law School, her eldest son, Roy, informed her that he would be putting his studies off for two years so that he could move to Israel and enlist in the military.

Goldstone, who was at a conference in Brussels at the time, could not believe his ears. He screamed at his wife over the phone, demanding that she lock Roy in his room until he could come back home and set him straight. Giving up a scholarship was an act of madness to him. When Ida told him he must respect his son's wishes, he accused her of breaking their status quo and undermining his authority as a father. For all intents and purposes, he blamed her for this event before hanging up on her.

When he returned, he found her in the kitchen, her chin in her hands, watching the snowy garden beyond the window. Without turning to face him, she said he had to remember that Roy was old enough to determine his own future.

Goldstone dropped his suitcase on the floor. "No fate, no divine intervention. It's only you and the crazy ideas you put in his head."

"My crazy ideas?" she said, standing up. "This is your fault!" she spat. "You and your exile complex, you and your obsession with power, with physical fitness. You may have wanted to toughen him up, but all you did was make him go off to Israel in search of his masculinity."

Goldstone pursed his lips and ran up to Roy's room. He found his son sitting on his bed, head lowered, nervously crushing the ends of his blanket. To Goldstone's question—whether he was willing to reconsider—he murmured that he was determined to enlist, and that no argument, as valid as it may be, could change his mind.

Holding back his anger, Goldstone said he fully respected his son's decision, and that all he asked for was a minor change to the schedule—getting his degree first, then enlisting. If Roy accepted this proposal, his father would reward him with a new car, a trip to Europe at the end of his freshman year, and a generous monthly allowance.

The boy refused, and Goldstone slammed the door behind him.

Ida transformed the dining room into a war room. She called the Israeli consulate and asked to speak to the military attaché. Then she called her cousin, who was assistant to the dean of the Columbia Law School, and asked that he find out if Roy could defer his scholarship for three years. Finally, she called Zvia, Goldstone's niece, who lived in Israel, and announced her son's imminent arrival. The cheers of joy on the other end of the line made Ida break into tears.

She never handled her children's absence well. The three weeks they spent at summer camp every year caused her insomnia. The thought of Roy being gone for three years was unbearable.

Yechiel, Zvia's husband, comforted her. Roy would be enlisting together with their eldest son, Alex. They would serve together. She could rest assured. Roy would have a warm, loving home in Israel.

When she brought up the idea of joining him in Israel for a few months, only until he got settled, Roy turned her down offhand.

"I'll do great with Aunt Zvia," he said. "Besides, someone needs to stay here with Dad."

She accepted the verdict, vowing not to break down—at least not in front of him. But a moment before he got on the plane, she buried her head in his chest and wailed.

Six months later, they all traveled to Israel for his swearing-in ceremony at the Wailing Wall. The family strolled through Jerusalem, marveling at the ancient stone houses, the blinding light, the bright colors, the fragrances of spices wafting over from the Arab market. Goldstone looked around, sweating, excited.

The Old City of Jerusalem was scarred with battle

wounds, but still gorgeous. When Goldstone was a child, his father used to tell him about the city, eyes burning. With the sensual longing of a lover, he described the mighty stone walls, the ancient castles, the towers, and the glorious Herodian temple rising over all. From a bird's-eye view, Goldstone could picture the pilgrims walking over from every corner of the land, the priests and Levites. In his mind, he heard flutes, harps, lutes. "Anyone who has never seen Jerusalem with his own eyes, has never seen a thing of beauty in his life," the dreamy rabbi repeated to his only son.

Now military bulldozers were clearing away rubble and rubbish from the ruins of the old Jewish quarter. Enormous dust clouds floated up into the evening sky, turning golden at the light of the setting sun. A fire inscription burned, and blue-and-white flags flapped in the wind. In the backdrop, the Moab Mountains turned red. A long, keening call to prayer undulated from the turrets of the mosques on the Temple Mount. A flock of pigeons rose over the walls with a flapping of wings, circling above their heads, soaring and swooping. Souls, he thought. The soul of his dead father, the souls of his mother and sisters, the souls of all Jews.

The orders of commanders and the obeying calls of soldiers reverberated from the mountains in the distance. Tears welled in his throat. He tightened his jaw and took a deep breath. *Calm and collected, man. Calm and collected.* He shut his eyes tightly, dimming the tears. When he opened them, he saw an enflamed, tan face before him. When he felt his son's strong, sweaty embrace, the tears broke loose.

Goldstone arrived at Fort Lauderdale Airport in a taxi he'd called from a payphone in the middle of the night. As the car raced past the largest settlement of elderly Jews in North America, he felt terribly shaky.

The journey from New York to Florida seemed endless, almost impossible, but Dr. Bartel's smug face on the front page of every morning newspaper ignited him with renewed determination. Exhausted, he closed his eyes and tried to relax. His heart was pounding, his blood pressure skyrocketing. A sharp pain spread through his temples. He had to survive, at any cost, to drag his destroyed body onward, all the way to the finish line. When he moaned with pain, the driver glanced back at him, eyes worried.

"Is everything all right, sir?" The man had beautiful, intense Arab eyes. They watched him from the rearview mirror, shaded under thick brows.

Goldstone smiled meekly. "Never better."

"You aren't going to die in my taxi, are you, sir?"

"Only if you ask me nicely."

The driver smiled, revealing pearly white teeth. "This is my first time driving outside of the city."

"I wish you the best of luck."

"I mean it, sir."

Goldstone raised a shaky hand. "So do I. Don't worry, I won't die here. Not today, anyway." His mouth filled with the bitter taste of humiliation. Helpless, dying old men like him had long ago lost their right to pass away among the living. He wished to say something defiant, but a severe cough blocked his throat.

"Seriously, sir."

"Calm down, man. I've got far more important things to do than drop dead in your taxi."

The driver nodded vigorously, embarrassed.

At this point, Goldstone became aware of the madness of his actions. His reflection in the rearview mirror revealed the wild gray hair, the burning eyes, the involuntary trembling of the facial muscles, the foam at the corners of his lips.

Newspaper headlines had announced that the prosecution would be seeking a life sentence without parole. Goldstone chuckled. A well-connected man like the defendant, who had given millions of dollars to charity, was the most precious commodity of every house party. The conviction had to be unequivocal, the kind that leads the suit-and-tie Nazi in a festive march toward the electric chair. He would get that conviction even if he had to crawl to the witness stand, spitting blood.

His children asked him to come join them in Florida as soon as the lung cancer was diagnosed. New York is a hard place for sick and lonesome Jews, they said, especially in the winter. "Come live near your family. Why not? You can freshen up your rusty Yiddish and meet lots of *shtetl* buddies. Have fun, lose your head. You deserve it."

Goldstone boiled over. "Lunatics!" he yelled at them. "Yiddish? *Shtetl?* Me? God, what obsession is this?"

Six months later, after a long series of radiation treatments, he was informed that he would be staying with them until he got back on his feet. They fattened him up almost by force and placed grandchildren on his lap: snot-nosed toddlers who wriggled like eels in his arms. They took photos of him holding the children from every possible angle, and announced that they wanted him close to them, close to the grandkids. "The children need their grandfather. How can you deny them that?" they rebuked.

When his patience ran out, he lashed out at them that, if he got worse, he planned to move to Europe.

"Europe?" they marveled. "Why Europe?"

"To die."

"Where, exactly?"

Their amused smiles only made him madder. "Any place would be good. Geneva, Zurich, Prague, Paris. Even Germany. Yes, come to think of it—Germany. They owe me big over there."

"After what they did to your family?"

He waved them off. "And what about the Polish? Did they not torment us? The Lithuanians? The Ukrainians? Was the Spanish Inquisition any better?"

"You can't compare those."

He had no scruples about German industry, neither when he bought himself a Mercedes, nor when he purchased Bosch appliances. "They owe us," he'd told Ida.

To tease his sons, he embarked on an evocative description of blond, buxom Bavarian nurses who would slather balm over his rupturing Jewish hemorrhoids. To prevent bedsores, they would gently turn him over from side to side like a rotisserie chicken. They would feed him applesauce with a silver spoon and wipe his mouth tenderly until he took his final breath. "You tell me—ultimately, what could be more comforting than the cool touch of a gray, mildewed stone above, as you lie on a damp bed of Jewish soil?"

His sons exchanged worried looks and nodded their agreement. Later, when his condition worsened, they admitted him to the Jewish hospital in North Palm Beach, an avant-garde, teardrop-shaped architectural eyesore in the heart of the sunny expanses of Florida.

Drenched in the pungent odors of sanitizer, urine, and ripe oranges, Goldstone accepted the fact that he would be counting down the rest of his days in the moronic march of aging.

The place was a goldmine: hefty inheritance resting on dry, sun-scorched skin, heavy makeup, Hawaiian shirts with abstract designs, wrinkled knees, smiles revealing enflamed gums, and flawless acrylic teeth. He imagined these sights would accompany him all the way to the grave—until, quite unexpectedly, the Jewish God of vengeance took mercy upon his soul, and dropped the last criminal case of his life into his lap.

The first time he called his New York office to ask who would be prosecuting the case, he was told half-heartedly that it would be led by his replacement, Dr. Donald Bartel, along with the new office team. Donald Bartel, a Georgia-born Republican, wished to complete one final term in peace before he retired to enjoy honor and glory in his spacious mansion in Wilmington, Delaware.

Next, Goldstone called Thomas Morton, the Attorney Generaland a close friend of his from graduate school. Agitated, Goldstone skipped the pleasantries and announced to Morton that he demanded to run point on the case.

With the Scandinavian languidness that he had perfected into an astute time-buying strategy, Morton asked, "First things first. How are you?"

"Dying."

"I'm very sorry to hear that."

"I'm very grateful for the sentiment."

"Honestly, Goldstone," he sighed, "I don't think this case would do your health any favors."

"Health? God, Morton. In my condition, nothing will improve my health. However, this case could certainly ease my suffering."

Morton paused for a long moment. "It's a bit more complicated than that," he intoned. "Donald has been dealing with this case for over six months. He's put in a lot of work. He says it's his life's project, that he—"

Goldstone cut him off. "Donald can't fill my shoes. Need I remind you that I have not handed in my resignation yet, nor have I been fired. Legally, I'm still on sick leave, and as far as you're concerned, I'm as healthy as a horse. I'm calling to let you know that I'm on my way to New York to take over the case.

Morton's voice sharpened into a scorched alto. "We have codes of conduct here."

"That's exactly what I'm talking about, Morton. Codes of conduct. And according to your goddamn codes of conduct, I am still the attorney general of the State of New York."

"Not exactly. You are incapacitated due to medical reasons."

"No incapacity procedures have been initiated. Therefore, according to the codes of conduct, I am still the attorney general."

"This case will kill you, Goldstone."

"Nothing can kill me any more than what's already killing me. You know I need this case."

"I can't have that on my conscience, Goldstone."

"I'm begging you."

"I don't know what to say."

"All you have to do is stick to the letter of the law. For the time being, there is no medical record on which to establish an incapacity claim. Issuing one can take months. Years, even. I'll talk to Donald, if you want."

"Oh, God, that's all I need. No, no, leave that to me."

"I want to hug you, Morton."

"You're making me feel like an executioner."

"I'll always remember this."

"Forget about it. Just make it work. I'm serving you my head on a platter, and there's quite a few people who would gloat."

"Worry not."

The next call he made was to Tony, his former housekeeper. Goldstone informed her that he was coming home for good.

She was surprised. "What? When?"

"I'll be home in about an hour. I'm going to stop by Wolf's for a Jewish bite. This trip destroyed me."

"Sir, are you sure that's a good idea?"

"What, going to Wolf's? What's gotten into you, woman?"

Tony laughed. "I mean coming back to New York. Your kids say you're very sick."

"I'm just fine, Tony. Can I ask you a favor?"

"You know very well you may."

"Could you move back in, just in case?"

Tony hesitated. She was sixty-two years old and devoted to her grandchildren. Her youngest son, Larry, was a handful. Goldstone had gotten him out of many legal entanglements over the years, and Tony was forever grateful to him. "You know I would, Mr. Goldstone, but I've got to be home for Larry's children."

"Is he in trouble again?"

"Oh, no, no, he's a good boy now. He's working very hard to pay back his debt and feed his children. Laura left him while you were gone. She left him alone with the kids. She—"

"If he's working, I can help him out. As for his children—I'll see what I can do. We can find a young girl to work as a live-in nanny. But I need you in my apartment. I need your help."

"Do your children know you're moving back?"

"They'll know, but I don't want them hanging around. They've got work, their own families. I can't accept that kind of sacrifice. You and I will do fine. Just like the old days, eh?"

Goldstone could hear her smiling on the other end. She was moved to tears. "Of course we will, Mr. Goldstone. We always have."

That afternoon he called the office and told Ms. Brown he was coming back to work. He asked that she have the casefile and all investigation materials on his desk the next morning.

Ms. Viola Brown, the office manager, was an aging British spinster, a visually impressive remnant of imperialism. She had a pinprick profile and a soft, doughy neck. When she heard his voice on the phone, she let out a startled cry. "Oh, Dr. Goldstone, is it really you? Are you feeling well?"

"No, Ms. Brown, I'm back from the dead. Is my office ready?"

The woman completely lost her cool. "The office? Wait, wait, just one moment please. I... I... I don't know, I must... let me check."

"Take your time."

"I'm afraid I have to inform Dr. Bartel of your arrival."

"You don't have to inform anyone," he growled. "In case you forgot, I'm still your boss, and I'd like my office to be available by tomorrow morning. And don't forget my orthopedic chair."

He walked into his apartment close to midnight. Tony was asleep on the old leather armchair, her head with its wreath of silver curls tilted at an angle, her mouth slightly open. She snored lightly.

The whack of the suitcase against the hardwood

floor startled her awake. When she saw Goldstone, she sighed with relief. Before she could voice an apology, Goldstone held a large, shushing finger against his lips. "Go back to sleep. We'll talk tomorrow."

The next morning, he found his clothes ironed and his shoes polished. The breakfast he'd had every morning for over thirty years was awaiting him in the kitchen: two sunny-side up eggs, a salad, and a slice of buttered toast. He took his coffee by the window in his study, as usual, watching the awakening street below.

Ms. Brown welcomed him with a sour smile. She tried in vain to imbue her voice with routine warmth, but her eyes bounced around, disclosing her discomfort. His gauntness was alarming, and his sunken eyes looked deranged.

Goldstone walked into his office and sighed as he plopped into his chair. Ms. Brown placed the case files on his desk, along with a cup of lemon tea and a piece of cake. Then she paused beside him and laconically reported the latest news in the same dry tone he'd spent years listening to. "Well, then, Dr. Bartel and three of our top attorneys have gone on indefinite unpaid leave. We have at our disposal four veteran staffers who would be glad to help with the case, along with two interns who have recently joined the office."

Goldstone listened with his eyes closed, nodding along. When she finished speaking, he instructed her to gather everybody into the conference room. "And when I say everybody, I mean everybody. No exceptions. We are going to win this case, Ms. Brown. At all costs!" When he was finished speaking, he coughed deeply into a handkerchief.

Two days later, Louie walked into Goldstone's office with urgency. Due to concerns about information leaks, delicate matters between the justice department and the DA's office were resolved only in one-on-one conversations. Louie Pirandello, personal assistant to the head of the justice department, was chosen for the mission.

Decisively, Louie reminded Goldstone that no one was contesting the fact that the defendant had made a dire error of judgment, one that could be interpreted in two contradictory ways. At any rate, the general assumption among the department's legal advisors was that this was an unfortunate but honest mistake, made of a desire to help the Jewish refugees. Additionally, the doctor was very contrite for the pain he'd caused the refugees in spite of his best intentions, and declared that he was prepared to suitably compensate any injured parties.

He added that the department of justice had an obvious interest in advancing any potential, fair, and discreet plea deal as quickly as possible, while completely keeping the media in the dark. Any leak would place responsibility exclusively on the shoulders of the DA's office.

Louie spoke in a low voice. The tan Sicilian's forehead muscles strove inward toward his skull in an effort to emphasize the gravity of the matter. "Put simply," he warned, "the justice department will not tolerate any attempt to push us away from our desired result.

What we need here is a quick and quiet plea, settled in private."

Goldstone glared at him. A new era. American justice fed intravenously with dollar bills. The defendant, intelligent enough, had made sure to grease the wheels of promising politicians on both sides of the political spectrum. The investment bore fruit. The man was a bipartisan consensus. All sides were in agreement with regards to the purity of his intentions. Several Republicans even submitted a bill for government funding for Dr. von Antrim's project. Such dangerous precedents made their way into law school textbooks. Before taking the bar exam, students had to memorize a growing list of laundered terms such as financial justice, political justice, and social justice. But Goldstone only knew one form of justice—piercing, perpendicular justice.

The late Professor Edward Gilbert, Goldstone's adored law school professor, had once made a typically British cynical remark about how what Americans consider to be absolute justice is, in fact, a marvelously elastic phenomenon, which could be stretched to infinity like the waistband on an old pair of boxer shorts, leaving behind—at most—a small, red, stinging mark on one's buttocks.

In other words, Goldstone was instructed to take good care of the Department of the Treasury's milking cow. Dr. von Antrim enjoyed the status of national treasure, and the strengthening relationship between the American government and the thriving West German Republic made him an even more unique diplomatic prized possession. Plea instructions had been delivered directly from the Oval Office. The arguments were fairly solid: First of all, it was all much ado about nothing. After all, no one died. Besides, barren women who could never afford expensive fertility treatments were now raising children.

Besides, what mass extermination were people referring to, for God's sake? The department's research found that the children were all healthy and more intelligent than average. Most of them received the finest Jewish upbringing. At most, this was an unfortunate human error stemming from pure motives.

Goldstone's expressionless face caused Louie to fall silent.

"I hope I've made myself clear."

Goldstone shook off his reveries. "Crystal."

Louie stood up and fixed Goldstone with a suspicious look. Then he grabbed his hat from the secretary's hands and took off. The espresso he had been served remained on the desk, still steaming. Goldstone downed it with a single gulp.

Blumenthal was a sentimental man with a rare tolerance for human deprivation. He cracked the hardest witnesses slowly, with immeasurable patience. His tone was apologetic as he sliced through the tough, sin-plumped stomachs of bitter criminals. His demeanor was as sweet as a priest taking confession as he liberated them from the weight of their scruples. With a skilled hand, he drained the inflamed abscesses of childhood, sanitized the bubbling rage, the old inferiority complexes, until a pleasant languidness spread through the bodies that were stiff with the terror of judgment day. For the first time in their lives, they felt clean, purified, blessed. They smiled to themselves even as they descended into the inferno to serve a life sentence.

Once the prosecution presented its claims, Blumenthal stood up in front of the jury and announced that the plaintiff, Ms. Erica Eisner, was no saint.

"Exhibit A," he called, waving a yellowing newspaper. "This article, published in a Munich daily paper a year before the plaintiff immigrated to the United States, covers a lawsuit filed against her for shooting to death the man who had saved her life during wartime. The lawsuit was withdrawn due to a lack of evidence."

Goldstone stood up. "Objection, your honor. Ms. Eisner's acquittal was accepted by every judge who ruled on her case. The defense's attempt to tarnish the plaintiff's reputation with an old legal affair that ended before it even began is a pathetic attempt to throw dust into the jury's eyes. I ask that this be stricken from the court records, and that the jury be instructed to disregard the exhibit."

"Sustained."

After the court was adjourned, Goldstone had Ms. Brown make an urgent appointment with Erica to review the deposition once more. She requested that they not meet in his office. "Anywhere you want," she said, "as long as it's outside."

John Macmillan's café was situated in a pretty cottage at the center of a public garden. A British village in the heart of the busy city. Pink and gold Victorian wallpaper, heavy oak furniture, and a library laden with England's greatest works of literature. Elegant old Upper East Side ladies in tweed suits and white gloves melted with pleasure when buttery scones accompanied their milky black tea in china cups, all served by waitresses speaking in lucid British accents.

John was a Black man of about sixty, a third generation descendant of slaves who fled to New York from the Jamaican sugar fields in the belly of a merchant ship. He was tall, with a broad face devoid of all wrinkles and a limp in his right leg—a painful souvenir from the Normandy landings. Twenty years earlier, Goldstone had gotten him off for the alleged murder of a white boy who had robbed him of his daily wages at gunpoint at the gas station where he worked.

John, the son of liberated slaves, didn't lose his cool. He punched the boy in the face and turned the barrel around. The boy pulled the trigger, tore an ugly hole in his own stomach, and collapsed. John called an ambulance and fastened a makeshift bandage to the boy's bloody wound in a desperate attempt to stop the bleeding. The boy died in surgery a few hours later.

This happened late at night in a desolate gas station on the outskirts of town. There were no witnesses. The boy's parents—wealthy farmers from Addison—claimed that this was murder in cold blood. "Billy comes from a good family," they told the media. "He wouldn't have robbed a gas station attendant. If he wanted money, all he had to do was ask." They added that he was a fine boy and a star athlete at his local college.

John's prospects were bad. His fingerprints were on the gun. The jury was comprised of white southern men who glared at him with hostility. The prosecution was seeking capital punishment.

Goldstone, then a no-name lawyer at the Birmingham, Alabama public defender's office, traveled to the dusty town to muster any evidence he could in John's favor. He came across a fortified wall of silence. But a beautiful intern he'd sent to the deceased's alma mater, undercover as a flighty visual art major, opened a can of worms that unlocked the boy's past. She discovered that he was a petty criminal who had gotten in trouble for stealing a gun from the sheriff's office and breaking and entering into liquor stores. These affairs were silenced through generous compensation paid by the family. The evidence she gathered was damning, and the jury had no choice but to fully acquit John.

Goldstone stretched his aching legs and sipped his coffee. The bitter flavor stung his tongue and he sighed indulgently, his taste buds converting the bitterness into a sense of delicate pleasure. He was still alive, after all. Grateful, he leaned his head back against his chair and dozed off.

His first conversation with Erica had been businesslike. The feminine voice on the other end of the line was stiff. Erica was determined to be the first on the witness stand. "First impressions matter. We have to condemn this man before the defense can manipulate the jury."

When she spoke of the child she had with William's sperm, Erica said that what was done was done, and though she could only speak for herself, she was completely convinced that each and every one of the women who had borne this Nazi criminal's children loved them just as much as any mother loved her kids.

When Goldstone asked if she could ever forgive him, she was silent for a long time.

"Forgive who?" she finally asked suspiciously.

"The defendant. Dr. von Antrim."

Erica's voice trembled when she said it was time to strike the word "forgiveness" from the Jewish dictionary. Her voice brimming with hate, she added that if she had the opportunity, she would have put the doctor to sleep like a sick dog, without a single pang of conscience.

Goldstone pulled her photo from the file folder and gave it a long look. Erica. A gorgeous woman beyond a doubt. A thrilling Semitic beauty, somewhat exotic. In spite of the fragile delicacy of her face, her gray eyes flickered with a dark, savage gleam.

When he glimpsed the colorful movement of her dress from the corner of her eye, he slipped the photo back into the envelope and turned toward her, smiling wide.

"Mr. Goldstone?"

He offered his hand. "At your service."

She took a seat across from him, allowing him to examine her face while she looked over the other diners. The old feminine trick warmed his heart.

When she asked him point blank what he wanted to discuss, he said that in spite of the detailed depositions she'd submitted to the court, there were still a few points that needed further clarification.

"By the way, what's his name?"

"Whose name?"

"The man you shot."

"Ulrich," she said. Then she added, disappointed, "I thought we'd put that behind us."

"It won't be brought up in court again, if that's what you're worried about. But the article presents you in a very negative light. A woman who murders her own savior in cold blood and is acquitted solely on the basis of insufficient evidence. It won't add any points in your favor."

Erica's face hardened. "He didn't save me from anything."

"I'm confused."

Erica became upset. "I don't see the point of these questions. That's still my claim against that article. I don't see how this could help me."

Patiently, Goldstone said, "You've got to understand that the jurors are simple folk. To hell with facts—they are moved by emotion. I'm convinced that telling them what happened from your own point of view will serve you well."

Erica described the event to him in great detail, which seemed to be intended to dull the powerful emotions still teeming beneath her buttoned-up exterior. Goldstone listened carefully. Like her, he was charmed by the pair of ancient Syrian chests in the lobby, the blue Ming vases, the black crystal chandelier which spread golden light on her family's living rooms during the salons her mother used to host. There was a black grand piano and wonderful paintings by Klimt, Modigliani, and Soutine. Up until the war, her family lived a tranquil bourgeois life. Her father, a professor of cardiology, ran the surgical department at a hospital in the city and worked as a part-time lecturer at a local university. Her mother was a concert pianist who had retired due to severe arthritis that distorted her knuckles and spent most of her time reading or playing bridge with her friends.

Her parents hired tutors who found Erica to be a smart, studious child, fluent in French and English. To her mother's disappointment, her musical ear was weak. But, on the other hand, she graduated from law school with flying colors.

The war began a year after that.

"Is this where Ulrich comes into the picture?"

"Ulrich was in the picture much earlier."

Ulrich was the only son of the Helbreiters, who had moved to Berlin five years before the war due to their financial straits, renting the apartment that had previously been occupied by the building's doorman, who had died earlier that year. The mother, a devout Protestant, knocked on Erica's family's door, offering up her services as housekeeper. The father was a blacksmith by profession and a zealous communist who worked as a janitor. When the mother fell ill, Ulrich dropped out of high school in order to help her with her job.

Erica recalled the blind, diabetic grandfather who always sat by the heater, warming his rotting legs, and treated Ulrich maliciously. His fat face glistened cruelly as he referred to Ulrich as a bitch, a sycophant, a maid. Whenever he sensed the boy walking past, he delivered a long barrage of insults. "We were horse groomers for the Hohenzollern dynasty for six straight generations, and look at you now, you little bitch, serving the Yids."

Ulrich never talked back, but his gloomy father would come to his aid from his spot in the corner. "And what exactly did you do there, you old fool? You spent two-hundred years chasing your own tails like idiotic peacocks in red courtiers' uniforms, shoveling horseshit."

The grandfather would sway from side to side, as if in lamentation. He rolled his dead, murky pupils before gargling with pride. "Better to shovel German horseshit than kike Jew shit."

Startled, Ulrich's father shushed him. "Papa, I'm begging you, be quiet. If anyone hears you, that'll be the end of us."

"Then shut your mouth. You're the one who brought us here."

Ulrich scrubbed toilets and said nothing. He cleared the rubbish from the kitchen and said nothing. He carried buckets of water, crates of vegetables, piles of laundry up to the roof, all in fuming silence. His movements contained an internalized rage. When spoken to, he responded curtly. When the questions were too invasive, he pushed them away with hostile wordlessness. Exhaustion got the better of him and he dozed off during night school for working boys. His grades were mediocre, and he failed his university entry exam.

Erica's father came to his aid, securing a scholarship for him at a law school. Ulrich was beside himself with joy. His father bowed before the professor, speechless. His mother collapsed in tears at the man's feet. His grandfather chuckled cruelly.

"A lawyer," he spat. Then he wondered out loud where the devout communist disappeared to whenever he heard the tapping of the Jewish capitalist's Italian leather loafers.

Erica and Ulrich did homework together, studied for tests together, and went out on the town together. To Erica, he was like a brother. It never occurred to her that he might have feelings for her.

"I didn't interpret his behavior as courtship," she kept repeating.

Goldstone raised a surprised brow. "How about your father?"

Erica made a face. "My father liked him a lot, but he never imagined we might become romantically involved."

"Did you love him?"

"I loved him like a brother. I never had any romantic feelings toward him."

"And you never had an inkling that he did?"

"By the time I realized it, it was already too late," she said. "Ulrich was a good guy, but very emotionally inhibited. He was always tender toward me. I couldn't tell anything was wrong until his fits of jealousy began."

"Fits of jealousy?"

"He got into an altercation with a boy who said something rude to me."

"I'd call that a gentlemanly gesture."

"It escalated to serious violence. The boy had stitches and broken ribs."

"Was he ever violent toward you?"

"Never!"

"What happened next?"

"Shortly before the war began, the family suffered one tragedy after the other. First, the grandfather died of a heart attack. Next, Ulrich's mother, who was a meek woman, contracted severe kidney failure, which quickly deteriorated into multi-system failure. My father was a doctor and he took dedicated care of them, free of charge. He also wanted to waive their rent, but

Ulrich insisted on paying. He picked up a second job at a printing house at night."

His grades deteriorated quickly. He barely made it to class, and when he did, he was much too tired to pay attention. It was only a matter of time before he started failing his exams. When Erica's father informed him that he planned to hire a new housekeeper, Ulrich panicked and asked the man to let him fill in for his mother until she got back on her feet. Her father refused outright. Ulrich's mother's chances of recovery were slim. Besides, Ulrich had to make use of the scholarship the man had secured for him and finish his degree.

At this point, Ulrich confessed his feelings for Erica. The doctor gaped at him, then murmured that Ulrich was being indecorous and ungrateful toward the man who had taken him in. He claimed this was crossing a line and shamelessly taking advantage of his daughter. He ordered Ulrich to put an end to it.

After a very belligerent exchange, Ulrich left Erica's father's office with his tail between his legs.

The week after that, his family moved out of their apartment and returned to the mother's home village, near Munich. She died just a few months later. Ulrich sent back Erica's father's letter of condolence, which included a generous check, without even reading it. He replied to Erica's letter with a brief thank you note. That was the last sign of life she received from him before the war. After that, they lost touch.

The last time they met was when she was raped in her office.

By the next day, he was dead.

"Do you remember the date of that night at the office?"

Of course she did. It wasn't the kind of thing one forgot. It was February 23rd, 1942, at 8:30 in the evening.

The day had started normally enough. It was colder than usual, and Erica wore a blue tweed suit and blue high heels she'd bought in Strasburg the previous year. Her taxi arrived at exactly 9 a.m. The night before, over the phone, she and Walter had agreed to have breakfast together.

Walter Remark was an old friend. They'd first met years earlier when she was a young intern at a law firm that had represented his business in Germany. He was a successful industrialist who had run a thriving agricultural machinery factory in Karlsruhe before recession and growing inflation led him to move his family to the United States. Erica was appointed to handle the liquidation of his German business and transfer of his factories to Michigan. Eight years later, after his wife had passed away and his children had moved out, he returned to Germany for a visit.

In the past, Walter had made several clumsy attempts at courtship, but Erica—then newly divorced—nipped the matter in the bud. "It won't work between us, Walter," she told him tenderly. "I'm not interested, and I like you way too much to lie to you."

At the sight of his painful expression she added that she loved him with all her heart, and that he was the best friend she'd ever had. Walter took her fingers in his hands and kissed them, one by one.

Now the taxi was late to drop her off. When she arrived, Walter was waiting, perusing the morning paper. She kissed his cheek and took a seat.

"You look very excited. I hope it's because of me."

Erica smiled affectionately. "It absolutely is."

"Want to tell me about it?"

"Are you familiar with Mayer and Hedwig Inc.?"

"Are you talking about Herman Hedwig, the steel mogul?"

"The same."

"I know him. We've done some business together. He's an honest and amusing man."

"I'm afraid he isn't amusing anymore."

"What does that mean?"

Erica smiled meaningfully. "He died in circumstances I would define as intimate. As for amusing, that depends who you ask."

"I remember him being a true gentleman."

"Herman was certainly an honest man. He lost his first wife at the age of sixty-seven—not a young man, but in excellent shape. No children. At one of his philanthropic events, he was introduced to the Countess Katrina von Antrim. Do you know her?"

Walter shook his head.

"Then perhaps you've heard of her uncle, Count Gustav von Antrim, a Wehrmacht general. Or her father, Count Kurt von Antrim, owner of the steel conglomerate Mayer Steel Industries Incorporated. He's the one who took out an enormous ad supporting the Führer on the front page of *Der Spiegel*. 'The Mayer Corporation will set Germany on steel legs.' Remember that?"

"I knew her father well. He had a good head for business. It was interesting: Hitler planned a war in secret, General von Antrim shared the confidential details with his brother, who rushed off to sign big fat deals with the Wehrmacht. Nothing new under the sun. War and business have always gone hand in hand. The odd thing is, the man didn't even bother to hide his connections. In fact, he took pride in them."

"You're right. It was the general's idea to merge the companies. In fact, neither Mayer nor Hedwig could have handled the contracts independently. The amount of product they had to supply for the German military was immense. If they hadn't merged, both companies would have lost their bids and would have likely gone under."

"And that's where you come in."

"Not exactly. They hired my ex-husband to handle the merger. But when his political involvement intensified, I took over the job. That's how I met Katrina and Herman Hedwig."

Walter chuckled. "And the love blossomed between them, naturally."

"At first, they suspected each other. Each side feared the other would try to take over, so we decided that the merger would be limited, only applying to Wehrmacht contracts. Later, when the collaboration turned out to be fruitful, I suggested they merge their businesses completely so as to avoid double taxation. Ultimately, their business relationship turned into a romantic one as well."

"Congratulations."

"Thank you. I worked hard on this."

When they finished eating, Walter lit his pipe and inhaled deeply. After a long silence, he asked, "Did you consider leaving?"

Erica was surprised. "Leaving?"

"Yes. Leaving Germany."

"My life is here, Walter," she said coolly. "This is my home."

Walter looked at her sternly. "Can't you see what's going on around you? Hitler is here to stay. It's becoming dangerous here, even for a German like me."

"A German like you? What's that supposed to mean?" she fumed. "Your grandfather, Louie, as far as I recall, was a Frenchman from Alsace. Your mother is a Polish woman from Silesia. My family, on the other hand, has been in Germany for over ten generations."

Walter exhaled a plume of blue smoke. "Your family could be here for a hundred generations, but you'd still be Jewish."

His words were like a punch in the face. "I'm being very careful," she murmured. "My firm is still registered under my ex-husband's name. I just need to get through this period. Hitler will be a brief episode. A small blemish on the face of German history."

"A brief episode?" he mocked. "Not while good people like you are creating a monstrous steel conglomerate to replenish his war machine. The partnership agreements you just signed with your clients aren't intended to provide the Wehrmacht with chamber pots. Isn't it high time you wake up?"

"And what exactly would you have me do?" she asked. "Shut down the firm? Flee to Switzerland like my parents? I'm trying to survive here. Everyone does business with the Nazis, even Jews. Even Applebaum's wholesale network sells to the Nazis, using brokers."

Walter shook his head. "Don't play naïve. You understand the difference between the two cases perfectly. Applebaum sells them food, not steel. And while we're on the subject of Applebaum, he isn't actually selling anything anymore."

"What do you mean?"

"He dissolved our contract a month ago. For twenty-two years, I supplied him with aluminum surfaces. He just told me he's sold his part of the business to his German partner so he can immigrate to Argentina. He isn't the only one, by the way. Fieselson and Gottfried also left the country."

"You mean Gottfried Weiller Textiles?"

"Exactly. He moved to Palestine a month ago."

"I had no idea they were having difficulties. They only recently opened a new store in Wilhelmstrasse."

"They're doing better than ever. They recently acquired a series of competitors who went bankrupt. They spent pennies and became a monopoly overnight."

"Strange timing, isn't it?"

"Perfect timing. Old man Gottfried might look senile, but he's very lucid. As soon as they became a monopoly, the company suddenly appeared very dangerous to the authorities. Hitler and his posse had their eyes on him. I heard that Gottfried and Weiller won an enormous military bid to supply uniforms and tents. The amount of money was unbelievable. Everybody knows Hitler has no intention of paying them one lousy mark, and that the only way the military can defer payment is by nationalizing the company. Mr. Gottfried realized he would be left empty-handed, so immediately after buying the companies and increasing the company's liquidity, he sold his portion to Weiller for a very fair price. For a tenth of that sum, he can recreate his textile empire in Palestine."

Erica smiled bitterly. "That's the difference between us," she said defiantly. "Mr. Gottfried can sell assets. I've got nothing to sell. Even my office is a rental."

Walter took her hands in his. "Leave everything and come with me to America. There's a large, established, sane German community in Milwaukee. Your expertise in international commerce will make you very popular. Let me help you, please."

Erica looked at him tenderly. "That's very kind of you, Walter, but I can't."

"Why not?"

"My entire life is here. I can't just get up and leave. I've got an obligation to my clients."

"To hell with your obligation!" Walter cried. "Your life is in danger, and you're talking to me about an obligation to *clients*?"

"I can't."

"I'm going to Zurich tomorrow, and from there flying back to the States. I'll leave you the address and phone number of my hotel in case you change your mind."

She returned to her office with a heavy heart. The hours ticked by slowly. In the late afternoon, it began to snow, the blizzard chasing people out of the streets. A loud knock came at the door, a slow, rhythmic pounding.

Everybody at the office froze. Erica signaled for them to get the door and took her seat behind her desk. She'd spent months waiting for the inevitable, yet somehow she was still surprised.

The S.S. soldiers walked in quietly. A tall figure pulled away from the line, crossed the hall quickly, and paused at the door to her office. It took her a long moment to recognize him.

"Ulrich?" Goldstone asked.

"Ulrich."

"Are you sure? Hadn't it been more than twelve years since you'd last seen him?"

"Not a doubt in my mind."

"But he must have changed, hadn't he? Such a long time had passed."

"He did change, but some things stay the same."

His blond hair was cropped. His boyish body had become heavier, firmer. But his mouth and eyes remained the same, except that the gaze had grown distant and hostile.

Erica got up from her seat. "Ulrich, it's me, Erica."

Not a muscle twitched in his face. Without turning his head, he spoke a quick command over his shoulder. The soldiers began to raid the office. Drawers were pulled out, their contents dumped on the floor. Shelving units laden with files tumbled to the ground. Documents flew through the air, crushed by wet boots. They weren't actually searching for anything.

"I've got a business license, if that's what you're looking for," she said, her voice trembling. "This folder contains everything: municipal payments, tax returns. I can make copies of anything you'd like. This destruction is completely unnecessary."

Erica had taken every precaution. Her husband's name still appeared on the bronze plaque on the front door as well as on every document that left the office. Classified documents were concealed in her parents' basement. She also had a forged baptism certificate, complete with the wax seal of Bishop Heinrich Griever of Kasseldorf. Heinrich, who had heart disease, had been her father's patient for years.

She must have been reported. Germans willingly reported their fellow civilians, not always out of the blinding power of hate, but sometimes in exchange for a sack of grain or potatoes. Often, they reported simply because they were asked to do so, and because they thought of themselves as law-abiding German citizens. She should have fled sooner. Now it was too late.

Jewish businesspeople with foresight had quickly dissolved partnerships with Germans and left the country. Her father, who had despaired of von Hindenburg and von Schleicher's failed attempts to unite the Social Democratic labor unions and the Christian labor unions in order to block the cancerous takeover of the mad Austrian corporal from Bohemia, tried to persuade her to leave with him and her mother to Switzerland until the danger of the war passed.

It had been her father who, two years earlier, had told off Dr. Manfred Lunz, his nephew, an eye doctor, for urging them to leave Germany with him before the ports closed. Her father had scolded the man with religious fervor, declaring proudly that he was a German and a son of Moses, who had participated in World War I as a military doctor, and had been decorated with an iron cross by General Erich Ludendorff himself. He would never dream of abandoning his homeland in its time of need.

Two years later, eyes lowered, he told her they could no longer trust the German law authorities—not because Hitler was breaking the law, but because he *was* the law.

Erica had refused. Her firm was thriving. Her husband's tangled international network of connections had allowed her to represent foreign companies and make a fine profit. By when Germany invaded Sudetenland and cut diplomatic ties with many European countries, many of them also severed their business relationships with German companies, which caused her great losses. Her relationship with her husband, which was already frayed, ended after an ugly infidelity on his part, which made it to the newspapers. Fortunately, they did not have children. As a central party member, he had to cut all ties with her so as not to hinder his meteoric rise to the top of the Nazi party.

He filed an expedited divorce plea and instructed his attorneys to meet all of her demands as long as she signed the divorce papers as soon as possible. At her behest, their shared assets were divided equally.

Ulrich clicked his heels and stood at attention. "Frau Abbet, opening a business is a crude violation of the law."

The sound of a metal file cabinet landing on the floor and her secretary letting out a sharp scream urged Erica to say, "Ulrich, please—"

Ulrich stamped his foot. "Frau Abbet, you may let your employees go. Untersturmführer

Schlenberg will handle the company's dissolution. I expect full cooperation from you." He raised his arm in a salute and left.

Goldstone ordered another cup of coffee and offered one to Erica as well. She politely declined. He sipped and asked, "Did Ulrich participate in the rape?"

"He wasn't there when it happened, but he knew all about it."

"And your employees?"

"They were told to go home."

"I see. And Schlenberg himself? Was he part of it?"

"He was outside."

Schlenberg, a Bavarian man in his thirties, had a round, flushed, childish face that stood in stark contradiction to his deep, husky voice. He placed his briefcase on Erica's desk and told her to sit down.

"Frau Eisner," he said graciously, "you'll have to sign some documents."

"What kinds of documents?"

"Documents resolving your ex-husband Herr Gustav Abbet's rights to your shared property."

Erica wrung her fingers until the knuckles turned white. "Gustav's rights had been resolved in an absolutely fair divorce settlement. Our shared property was equally divided, and he signed the documents out of his free will."

Schlenberg's face fell. "Frau Eisner, Herr Abbet has been disinherited from his family assets, and you must sign the waivers."

"What are you talking about?"

Schlenberg placed a piece of paper on the desk. "I'm talking about the apartment given to you by your ex-husband's parents."

Erica's lips trembled. "The apartment was falling apart when we got it," she said, her voice wavering. "My parents paid for the renovation. They also gave us a generous monthly allowance for the first five years of our marriage. Their assistance cost much more than half the apartment. And at any rate, my ex-husband is the one who suggested registering the apartment under both our names."

"The apartment is the property of a German citizen. Legally, you cannot possess it."

"*I'm* a German citizen."

Schlenberg pushed the paper toward her. "Frau Eisner, I suggest you sign willingly. Believe me, we have much less pleasant ways of making you do it."

Erica hesitated a moment before picking up the pen and signing with a shaking hand. When she was finished, Schlenberg examined the signatures carefully before slipping the paper back into his briefcase.

With a flick of his wrist, he swept her desk clear, sending items clanging onto the floor.

Erica turned white.

Schlenberg gestured toward the desk. "Now if you'll please be so kind as to undress and lie down on the desk. You'd best leave your clothes on the chair. I don't suppose it would be wise of you to resist. These boys tend to be very violent when they meet resistance."

Lying naked in a strange bed, covered with a woolen blanket that stank of sweat, Erica woke up into absolute darkness. Her head was pounding with pain and there was a sharp burning sensation beneath her belly. She reached a tentative hand down and found she was still bleeding.

A green reading lamp lit up at the corner of the room and a dim male figure suddenly rose from his seat. The man's perspiring face glistened like a copper relief. His voice reached her as if from a distance.

"You're awake." The words were accompanied by a monotonous ringing that struck her ears.

Erica rose to her elbows.

"Rest." It was Ulrich's voice.

"Where am I?"

"Someplace safe."

"Where?"

"My apartment. There's a glass of water and some painkillers on the bedside table."

She let herself fall back onto the bed. Every breath hurt her ribs. She pursed her lips and cried silently. Then she swallowed down a painkiller and went back to sleep.

She woke up again three hours later, her temples still throbbing with pain. Nauseated, she tried to sit up. The bitter taste of congealed blood filled her mouth.

Ulrich said, "Try to get some rest."

"My head hurts."

"Schlenberg told me you put up a fight."

Tears streamed down her face. The last thing she remembered was the sadistic smile of a pockmarked blond man who pinned her against the desk and wrapped his fingers around her jaws, pulling her mouth open in order to empty a bottle of cognac into it. She spat the drink in his face, and he slapped her. When she scratched his cheek, he hit her on the head with the bottle.

She couldn't remember anything after that.

"Was Schlenberg there?" she asked.

"What do you care about Schlenberg?"

"I want to know."

"He saved you."

"*Saved* me?" she cried. "He was the one who suggested I get undressed so that my clothes didn't get torn up."

"No one could have prevented what happened, but you're alive thanks to him."

"I guess I'm supposed to thank you for that, too."

Ulrich's face twisted into a spiteful smile. "You'll get your chance, I assure you."

They had been five men who punched her in the head and chest. Each time she passed out they slapped her awake. Schlenberg told them he would transfer her to headquarters for a follow-up investigation. He pushed them off her. Then he covered her naked body with his jacket and brought her to Ulrich's apartment.

A burning sensation and pressure in her lower back reminded her she had to use the bathroom. Wrapped in a blanket, she swayed across the room, toward the dark hallway. She felt dizzy. When he reached his hand for her, she recoiled.

"I'll manage on my own," she said.

When she returned, she sat down on the bed again, shaking.

Ulrich got up, pulled a bottle of whiskey from the sideboard, and poured it into two glasses. "Drink," he said.

The whiskey burned her throat, then spread a warmth through her. She handed him the empty glass and he refilled it. This time she sipped it slowly until she stopped shaking. "So I'm supposed to thank you for saving my life."

Ulrich examined the yellowish brown liquid in the lamplight. "You might say that."

"Why didn't you kill me? I signed all the documents."

"Your ex-husband did instruct us to kill you immediately after you signed. You're still alive because I haven't gotten what I want from you yet."

Rage spewed from her mouth. "What is it you want from me, Ulrich? You want to fuck me? You want to rape me like Schlenberg's filthy gang? Just tell me now—what is it you want?"

"I want you to do a little something for me."

She wanted to yell at him, but recalled she was penniless. She'd lost her home and all her possessions.

Even her clothes were gone. She had to convince him to take her back to her apartment so she could pack up some clothes and a few sentimental items. Then she had to get to the bank as soon as she could. It would take at least a week for Schlenberg's transfer of ownership documents to take effect. For the time being, she was still the apartment's legal owner. She had quite a bit of cash in her bank account. Some savings, some mutual funds, some bonds. She would need lots of cash if she was going to get out of there and start a new life in Switzerland. The new regulations limited the amount of money Jews were permitted to carry out of the country, but the firm's bank account was still listed under her husband's name, and he was a party member. It would take a simple phone call for Frau Heller, her office manager, to transfer all the money in the account to her father's bank in Switzerland.

"If you want to leave," Ulrich said, "you'll have to do something for me first."

Erica looked at him in silence.

The light from the heater set his face aflame. A hateful smile hovered over his thin lips. "Did you ever love me?" he asked.

"So, we're talking about love now?" Erica got up slowly, letting the blanket fall away. Naked, bleeding, trembling with weakness, she opened her arms. "Come to me, my love," she said mockingly. "Take me."

"Stop it."

"You want me to hold you? To whisper in your ear that I loved you, that I've always loved you, only you, is that it?"

His sweaty face crumpled. "*Stop it.*"

"It's difficult, my love," she whispered sweetly. "It's difficult to see me like this, isn't it?" She opened her arms again. "Look at me now. Take a good look at your beloved Erica. Think about what your filthy friends did to me, one after the other, for a whole hour. Are you listening? They befouled me for an entire hour."

Ulrich shut his eyes tight.

"Is that difficult, my darling? Is it hard to hear? You're so sensitive."

All of a sudden, he got up and took hold of her shoulder. "How could you have let him?" he asked. "How could you have let your father kick us out to the street?"

"You're hurting me."

Ulrich let go and Erica retreated and collapsed onto the bed. Ulrich came closer. "Forgive me," he cried. He fell to his knees and buried his head in her lap. "Forgive me, forgive me. I'm a bad man," he said, taking her hand and resting it on his face.

"You've done bad things, Ulrich."

"I'm a bad man." Then, as if he fathomed the meaning of his own words, he added hoarsely, "Dear God, I'm a great sinner."

"What have you done, Ulrich?"

A new wave of tears shook the large body. He gripped her thighs. "I've murdered." He looked up at her, his face drenched with tears. "I ought to be punished." Then he sprung to his feet. His eyes gleamed. An innocent smile spread over his face. Ulrich's tender soul beamed from within his wet complexion. The image of the little boy he used to be, a devout Christian with stiff flaxen hair and that heartbreaking gap in his teeth, appeared for a flash before vanishing again. The diabolical smile returned. "If you want to leave, you're going to have to do something for me," he said again.

Erica tried to buy some time. "We're both exhausted. Why don't we talk tomorrow morning—"

"There isn't going to be a tomorrow."

A tremble ran through her back. "Are you going to kill me, Ulrich?"

"I don't want to kill *you*." He laughed madly.

The meaning of this slowly sank in. "You want to... die?"

"Not exactly, but keep going," he urged her.

"You want somebody else to kill you?"

He nodded.

Erica could hardly breathe. "Me? You want me to kill you?"

"You're going to help me."

"I can't do that!"

"It isn't up to you."

"You're mad! I won't do it."

"You've got no choice."

"I'll forgive your sins if you just help me get out of here."

Ulrich held her to his body. His face filled her field of vision, losing its form. His eyes ran all over her face. "I could rape you, I could hurt you, I could humiliate you. I'll do whatever it takes to make you hate me," he hissed.

Erica tried to push him off. "Let me go!"

He shook her shoulders violently, spraying her with his spit. "Stop lying to me, damn it! You'll never be able to forgive. Do you have any idea what I've done? How many people I've murdered? This is your opportunity to execute a monster. Take it, and you'll be free to go." He threw her on the bed. "You've got no choice."

"And if I say no, what then? Will you kill me?"

He turned away from her. "No," he said, his back to her. "I'll just turn you in to the Gestapo."

"You wouldn't turn me in."

He turned to face her again. Without a hint of hatred in his voice, he said, "I will." Then he plopped into his chair and closed his eyes.

"I won't do it," she declared. "You won't turn me into a murderer like you."

Ulrich smiled meekly. "One hour in the Gestapo basement in Oranienburgerstrasse and you'll curse missing the opportunity to split my head open with a hammer."

Erica got up from the bed and looked around for her clothes.

"You won't find them," Ulrich said. "You came here wearing nothing but Schlenberg's raincoat."

Erica paused in the center of the room. "How will I get out of here?"

Ulrich pointed at the closet. "Everything's on the shelf in there. You can take a shower, too. There's hot water."

In the closet, Erica found a carefully folded S.S. uniform and a long-hanging raincoat. On the bottom shelf was a pair of black, women's flats and black pantyhose. Whoever had procured this knew her exact measurements.

She was surprised to find her makeup case in the bathroom. "How did this get here?"

"Schlenberg brought it from your office. I imagined you would need it."

"Does Schlenberg know about your plan?"

"Schlenberg is just following orders. When you finish getting dressed, leave the building through the emergency exit. He'll wait for you downstairs until no later than 5:30. At the St. Gallen border crossing, he'll provide you with passage papers, civilian clothing, and a bit of money. You can take a shower now. I'll wait here in the chair."

She scrubbed her skin vigorously. Her wounds burned and blood ran from her broken nose, bubbling against the white tiles. When she was finished she got dressed, pulled back her hair, and applied some makeup. Then she opened the door a crack. Ulrich appeared to be asleep. Carrying the shoes in her hand, she tiptoed to the door, which she found to be locked.

Ulrich's voice came from behind her back, low and contemptuous. "You thought you could leave without delivering your part of the deal?"

"Let me go."

"We made a deal."

"We did no such thing."

"You have to."

When she turned to face him, he was fixing a silencer onto a gun. His face was tranquil.

Her knees buckled. "Let me go, Ulrich. It's already ten past five."

"Do it, and in a few hours you'll be across the border and free."

Erica reached out her hand. "Give me the key before it's too late."

Ulrich raised his left hand. He was pinching a copper key between thumb and forefinger. "It's up to you, my darling." He moved the key closer to her.

Erica reached for it when, all of a sudden, Ulrich grabbed her hand and pulled her in. His arms gripped her body, hard. When she tried to punch him, he wrapped his legs around her body, his right hand pinning her head to his chest.

"Two seconds, my love," he whispered into her ear. "Just devote two seconds of your life to your Ulrich."

Erica wriggled and pierced her fingernails into his arm. When she screamed, he squeezed tighter and covered her mouth with his hand. "Shut up! You're only putting your own life at risk. I'll be out of this whole filthy debacle in a few minutes."

Erica cried. When he removed his hand from her mouth, she muttered, "I'll never do it. Never."

He laughed venomously. "You'll do it, Erica, whether you want to or not. You'll kill the rabid dog with your own hands." He pulled open her fists, wrapped his hand, which held the gun, around hers, and shoved the barrel into his mouth. Then, with determination, he pulled the trigger.

Silent tears ran down Erica's face.

"Meaning," said Goldstone, "that he was the one to ultimately pull the trigger."

"I don't know. I lost sensation in my fingers at that moment."

But she did remember the thrust of the gunshot, the shock that rocked Ulrich's large body, and the complete loosening that followed. The awful sight of the gaping, empty eyes, and the mocking smile that congealed over his dead face. All of these were etched into her mind forever.

"You shouldn't blame yourself."

Erica buried her face in her hands. "I pulled the trigger."

Goldstone shook his head. "What ultimately killed him was his own tortured conscience," he said decisively.

"I don't know."

She released herself from the grip of the dead arms and got up, trembling all over. From behind the door, she heard footsteps moving away. She had to get out of there as quickly as possible. Searching frantically for the fallen key, she spotted her own image on his bedside table. She recognized herself immediately—a girl of fifteen, riding a horse through a field. Beside her, holding onto the bridle, was Ulrich, a lean boy with a bashful smile and veiled eyes.

She walked into the bathroom and fixed her smeared makeup with shaky hands. Then she walked out of the apartment, locked the door behind her, and ran out of the building.

Schlenberg's car was waiting on the corner, headlamps off. He signaled to her with a quick flashing of the lights.

When she got in, he asked, "Did you lock the door behind you?"

"Yes."

"Did you turn out the lights?"

"I did."

He nodded, pleased. "And you're sure he's..."

"Dead. He's dead."

"You know, he might only be injured, even badly injured, but—"

"He's dead. As dead as can be. He shoved the barrel into his mouth and shot."

"Did anyone see you coming out? Did you hear anything?"

"I think I heard someone behind the door. I'm not sure. I can't remember anything." She paused. "Were the two of you friends?"

Schlenberg looked at her askance, his thin eyebrows rising with surprise. "Friends? Not at all. Ulrich was my commander."

"Did you know he planned to kill himself?"

Schlenberg drove fast.

At 11 a.m., they arrived at the St. Gallen border crossing. A long line of military cars and trucks ambled slowly down the road leading to the security check near the camp. Two rows of barbed wire fences surrounded the area, two watchtowers near the entrance, metal blockades all along the road, and armed soldiers accompanied by dogs patrolled the site every hour of the day and night.

The wind picked up. Loose tarps on military trucks whipped the air. A heavy rain began to fall.

Schlenberg pulled up by the camp gate and gave a short honk. An armed guard in a long coat and earmuffs walked cheerlessly out of the heated booth, rubbing his hands and blowing on them for warmth. A guard dog scampered near him, baring its teeth and growling menacingly. The guard looked at their papers and pointed at one of the buildings.

"Headquarter offices are in there. You can get your passage papers signed inside. No point to keep going after that, the blockade will only open in two hours. In the meantime, you can park in the guest lot. If you plan on spending the night, register with the commander on duty to arrange beds for you. In the meantime, you can grab something to eat at the officer cafeteria and rest in the guard room. It'll be free for the next three hours, until the soldiers get back from their patrol."

"Thank you," said Schlenberg, "but there will be no need. I'm going back, and the Hauptsturmführer will continue to Switzerland."

He got out of the car and pulled a small suitcase from the trunk. The two of them walked silently toward the guard room, where they were welcomed by a cloud of dank air. Twelve perfectly made foldable cots were lined up against the wall. An iron heater stood in the center of the room, a sooty metal samovar humming on top of it. An open packet of biscuits rested on the desk. A lamp illuminated the derelict setting with yellow light.

Schlenberg put the suitcase down on the desk and opened it. "You've got a few days' worth of civilian clothing in here. Immediately after you cross the border, go to the bathroom and change." He placed a manila envelope on the desk. "You'll find new certificates here, a one-time passage license, and some money." He handed her a different envelope. "Destroy these."

"What's in there?"

"The transfer of ownership documents you signed last night. Destroy them immediately."

Erica shivered. Ulrich had kept his promise. The mocking smile on his dead face flickered before her eyes again. Loathing. Disdainful. "Could you please do it?"

Schlenberg opened the small window in the iron heater and pushed the envelope through it. The flames consumed the papers in an instant.

The ruckus of trucks entering the camp startled her. "Don't you think we'd best go now?"

Schlenberg glanced out the window. Lines of vehicles stood on the shoulder of the road. Passengers waited on platforms. It snowed ceaselessly. "Best to wait for dark," he said. "Draw as little attention as possible. You don't need to worry, your papers are of the highest quality. If any issues come up, ask to see the station manager on the Swiss side. His name is Paul Groninger. He'll help you."

Schlenberg flipped through an old newspaper on the desk while Erica paced the room restlessly. An hour later, they drove down to the border crossing. Cars were starting to go through.

"I don't even know your first name," said Erica.

Keeping his eyes on the road, Schlenberg said drily, "I think we've managed just fine without it so far."

"I'd like to thank you."

Schlenberg shook his head. "Ulrich is the one who saved your life."

"He was going to turn me in to the Gestapo."

Schlenberg looked at her pointedly. "Ulrich *was* the Gestapo. He started planning your rescue as soon as he received your casefile—"

A brief honk cut him off. An indecipherable announcement was made over the loudspeakers.

"You'd better leave now," said Schlenberg. "If the roads become snowed in, you'll get stuck."

"Whatever happened to Schlenberg?" Goldstone asked.

"He was caught back in the apartment, where he returned to get rid of the evidence. One of the tenants had called the police. Schlenberg had managed to wipe my fingerprints off of the gun before he was caught, and that's what saved me from being incarcerated. He was tried, indicted as an accessory to murder and betrayal, and executed at the Gestapo facility in Berlin. When I returned to Germany after the war, Ulrich's family sued me for murder."

"A lawsuit in which you were ultimately acquitted due to lack of evidence."

"Correct."

Goldstone lit a cigarette. "Your file mentions you spent three weeks at a psychiatric hospital in Zurich, ten months after arriving in Switzerland."

"I was hospitalized after I gave birth."

"Meaning you got pregnant as a result of the rape?"

Erica nodded.

The morning sickness began about six weeks after her arrival at her parents' home in Switzerland. It never even occurred to her that she might be pregnant, and by the time she found out, it was too late to do anything about it.

Her parents were vehemently against getting an abortion anyway. "The baby is innocent," they told her. "It isn't the baby's fault."

"Your parents?" Goldstone marveled.

"My mother defended the fetus. She said it was a kosher Jew."

"So, they knew about the rape?"

Of course they knew. She'd seen no point in trying to hide it. She'd told them everything as soon as they were reunited. The news had destroyed them.

"Did you want the kid?"

"No!" she said. "I was so scared he would look like one of them. I was scared I'd hate him."

"But you had him."

"I did."

When they placed the baby on her chest, screaming, wriggling, covered with blood, she was gripped with such intense anxiety that the doctors had to inject a sedative. She suffered severe postpartum depression and was hospitalized in a closed psychiatric ward. After that, she spent two months in a private sanatorium near Basel while her parents cared for the baby. In their lonesomeness, the child became the center of their lives. He was a cheerful, gorgeous creature who spread golden magic over his surroundings. While she was dying on the inside, her parents were filled with renewed vitality.

They read him the same old books they used to read to her. They sang him the songs she knew by heart. Her mother, who had abandoned the piano years earlier, now sat the child on her lap as she spent hours playing for him. She beamed with joy when she informed Erica that her son had perfect pitch. The day she heard the boy refer to his grandmother as "Mama," Erica decided to go to America and start over.

"Without him?"

"Without him. That was the greatest gift I could give him. He called me 'Aunt Erica.' Every time I looked at him, I remembered his father's hands on me, and then even his innocent eyes would become sinister. That's what did me in." Erica's eyes welled up.

"So I take it your parents are still raising him?"

"My father passed away two years ago. My mother is caring for him on her own."

"How old is he now?"

"Ten."

"And your mother?"

"Sixty-nine."

"Is she not too old to raise a ten-year-old?"

Erica flushed. "My mother is young at heart, healthy. She's perfectly functional."

"Does he know you are his real mother?"
"It's too early."
"Aren't you worried about his reaction?"
Erica sipped her coffee. "Of course I am."
"How is your relationship with him?"
"Like a loving aunt's. He visits me on holidays and during summer vacation, staying for longer stretches every year. Once my youngest is a little older, my eldest will be able to stay with us for good..."

"Your youngest. Are you talking about Dr. von Antrim's son?"

"I'm talking about *my* son."

B**lumenthal** refused to object to the corrected lawsuit. As an experienced attorney, he believed that Goldstone's revisions, which charged the defendant with a new, more severe accusation—attempted genocide—delivered the prosecution into new heights of absurdist comedy, which would come crashing down at the pounding of the judge's gavel.

Blumenthal paused a distance away from the witness stand. Facing the jury, he fired his questions at Erica.

"Name?"

"Rebecca Hacohen Eisner."

The attorney shook his head. "Ms. Erica Elizabetha Eisner was born in Berlin on September 5th, 1919. Thus states the plaintiff's birth certificate. Let the record show that the name of the witness is Erica, not Rebecca."

The next exhibit was a notarized document with a red wax seal. "Exhibit fifty-four, marriage certificate of Ms. Erica Elizabetha Abbet. Would you please tell the court who Mr. Abbet is?"

"My ex-husband."

"Please state his full name."

"Dieter Rudolf Abbet."

"Jewish?"

Goldstone raised his hand, but the judge beat him to the punch.

"Sustained."

Blumenthal backed off. "Do you recognize the man sitting at the defendants' table?"

"I do."

"Would you be so kind as to tell us who he is?"

"He is Dr. William von Antrim."

"Did the defendant provide you with medical care?"

"He did."

"Did you pay for this care?"

"I wanted to, but—"

"Did you or did you not?"

"He refused to—"

"Did you or did you not pay for this care?"

"I did not."

"Meaning that, ultimately, you received fertility treatments free of charge."

Erica nodded.

"Please speak up, ma'am."

"I received the treatment free of charge."

"Thank you. Were you experiencing financial difficulties at the time?"

"No, my financial situation was rather good."

"Meaning, you received expensive medical care for free from the defendant."

"That's right."

Blumenthal sipped from his water glass. "Was Dr. von Antrim's treatment successful?"

"Eventually."

"In other words, there had been some unsuccessful attempts?"

"Correct."

"How many rounds of IVF did you go through?"
"Seven."
"Did you pay for any of these?"
"No."
"Did you voice any reservations to Dr. von Antrim with regards to the donor's identity, his origins, his racial, religious, or ethnic identity?"
"I asked that the man not be Jewish."

Blumenthal hooked his thick thumbs through his belt loops. He paced in front of the witness stand, thoughtful. "Due to a concern over potential bastardism according to Jewish law?"

"Yes."

"Meaning that, as far as you were concerned, as long as the donor wasn't Jewish, you wouldn't care if he was Black, Indian, or Asian?"

"Dr. von Antrim assured me that the donation was taken by people who have as similar physical qualities as possible to those of the parents."

"Meaning, that as far as you were concerned, the donor could have been any non-Jewish white male?"

Erica hesitated.

"Please answer the question, Ma'am," Blumenthal barked.

"I suppose so."

"The court does not deal with suppositions, Ma'am."

Goldstone raised his hand. "Objection, your honor. This was a hypothetical question, in which case the witness can only answer to the best of her knowledge."

Blumenthal turned to the judge. "Your honor, the defense is attempting to clarify the rationale that preceded the witness's decision to go ahead with the fertilization treatment. Her judgment is of utmost importance in proving my client's innocence."

"Overruled."

"I'll repeat the question. Did you voice any other reservations regarding the donor, assuming he was white and non-Jewish?"

"I certainly wouldn't have agreed to have a German donor."

Blumenthal placed a piece of paper on the witness stand. "Exhibit fifty-five. Do you recognize this document?"

"I do."

"Would you please tell the court what it is."

"This is a document confirming my consent to treatment."

"That's correct. This document explicitly states an undertaking to secure a maximal match between the donor and the patient. On the bottom, you can clearly see your objection to a Jewish donor, as well as your signature. Did you mention an objection to a German donor in this document?"

Erica blushed. "That should go without saying."

Blumenthal held his glasses to the light, then wiped them meticulously on the ends of his robe. "Isn't it odd to hear such vehement objections from a woman who was once married to a senior member of the Nazi party? A woman who, under different circumstances, could have been a mother to German children?" he asked.

Goldstone raised his hand. "Objection, your honor.

The witness's past marriage to a German man does not hinder her right to choose her sperm donor."

"Sustained. Mr. Blumenthal, please move on to the next question."

Blumenthal lowered his head. "In your deposition, you said you were worried that a son born of Dr. von Antrim's sperm might grow up to become a murderer."

"Almost every mental illness has a genetic component."

Blumenthal turned to face the jury. "There is no mention of mental illness in my client's medical records."

Spitefully, Erica said, "His father, the murderer, was executed for committing crimes against humanity. If he is not insane because of mental illness or severe disturbance, that means the man slaughtered hundreds of thousands of Jews willfully, and of sound mind."

Blumenthal stared into the air. His voice had become ponderous. "Do you believe that human evil is hereditary?"

Goldstone raised his arm. "Objection, your honor. The witness has expressed her decisive objection to receiving a sperm donation from an indicted war criminal. She is not here to make scientific observations."

"Sustained. Mr. Blumenthal, please move on to the next question."

Blumenthal raised his hands. "Your honor, the defense rests."

Goldstone had inherited his resentment and sense for revenge, which would end up slowly ruining him, from his father. At least, that's what his wife, Ida, had told him.

It started years earlier: Polish drunks, led by Andrzej, the owner of a tavern in a village outside of Bialystok, beat up Laser Halberstam, the young son of the revered rabbi of Tarnow, when he came to collect a debt in the amount of four-hundred zloty. They beat the young liquor merchant half to death, tearing off his clothes, chopping off his sideburns, pushing him to the floor, and punching and kicking him until he lost consciousness. The wallet in his pocket, which contained three-thousand zloty, had remained untouched.

Laser lay in a hospital bed for weeks with a severe concussion, fractures in his left leg, and a torn spleen. His elderly mother sat beside him, mumbling Psalms, her eyes closed. Every so often, she picked up a wet sponge and moistened her youngest son's chapped lips.

When he was released from the hospital, hobbling on crutches, Laser struck a new deal with Andrzej's father for the sale of a thousand gallons of liquor to the tavern. Andrzej shook Laser's hand tenderly.

Rabbi Isar Alter Goldstein, Goldstone's father, could not stand the disgrace. He stormed into the hospital room, dragging his startled son, Daniel, behind him. Daniel's mother had protested, but his father insisted. "This visit is meant to teach him about Jewish pride," he told her.

Laser was lying in bed, supported by pillows, his left leg hanging in a cast, his right arm in a splint, and his head wrapped in bandages. He greeted his guest with a contemptuous smile. "To what do I owe this honor?"

Rabbi Isar Goldstein waved the question away. "Honor? Obligation is more like it. I don't understand how you could have forgiven him. How could you have kissed the hand that beat you?"

"Forgive?" the injured man asked. "What are you talking about? Who forgave anybody?"

"The whole town is talking about the deal you made with Andrzej, the man who tried to murder you."

Laser smiled cunningly. "Good lord, Rabbi Goldstein," he said, his voice appeasing. "What did you expect me to do? Beat him? Turn the hands of Jacob into the hands of Esau?" Then Laser touched the rabbi's hand and said affectionately, "It's no big thing. A stray dog just bit my hand."

"One ought to keep their distance from stray dogs," said the rabbi.

Later on, Goldstone's father became enamored with Zionism. In hiding, he began reading the works of Rabbi Samson Hirsch, Rabbi Abraham Kook, and Rabbi Samuel Mohilever. His dream of immigrating to Palestine had turned into a feverish obsession. When the pogroms began, he started preaching *Aliyah* at the synagogue, the market, the *mikveh*, and anywhere else where Jews congregated.

His objectors protested with cries of "*gevald*," slamming their fists on tables. When people began following him, things became heated. Posters calling for a boycott were pasted on walls all over town. He called them blind fools who refused to see the signs of approaching redemption.

Goldstone remembered vividly how a rock had shattered the window of their home on a Friday night, rolling onto the white tablecloth on the dinner table, destroying the expensive china dowry. He remembered the horror in his mother's eyes. But when he tried to toss the rock back at the rioters, his father stopped him with a pointed finger.

"Don't touch that," he said. "It's Shabbat."

Eventually, they were all killed during the great pogrom.

Years later, Goldstone described this event as "the dress rehearsal before the great fire at the Auschwitz purgatory."

He was the only survivor. Tekla, the family's Polish servant, had saved him from the killing fields. She was only twelve years old when she began helping his sickly mother with the housework. When the children were born, she became a governess. When they grew up, she became a housekeeper, and the family's ultimate rule maker.

She was a taciturn woman, tall, robust, with a crude, flushed face, blue eyes, and a thick blond braid wrapped around the top of her head. When the pogrom started, she was on her way back from a visit to an elderly aunt who lived in a nearby village. As she walked down the street carrying baskets, she saw a parade of excitable drunks making its way back from the Jewish neighborhood. Their clothes were blood stained, their arms laden with clothes and housewares. Some of them were dragging carts behind them, loaded with a mess of appliances, furniture, sacks of flour and potatoes.

Ominous plumes of heavy smoke swirled over the neighborhood houses. She dropped the baskets to the ground and broke into a run, but soon enough she realized she was too late. The bodies of her employers lay out in the yard, wallowing in puddles of blood, terror congealed upon their faces. She quickly ran her eyes over the murder scene. The rabbi, his wife, and their two daughters were all there. Only Daniel, the youngest child, the apple of her eye, was missing.

Growling with madness, she ran into the house, freezing when she heard the loud sounds of drawers slamming up in the nursery. The murderer was still in the house.

She tiptoed into the kitchen, grabbed a serrated meat knife, and climbed stealthily up the stairs. Through the half-open door, she saw the man kneeling on the ground, patiently sorting items. There were two piles in front of him, and every once in a while he held an object up to the window and looked it over carefully. Daylight streaming into the room lit up the intruder's face. She recognized him immediately—Juliusz the cattle merchant. The elegant mustard jacket he wore every Sunday was lying beside him, stained with a great deal of blood, a bloody butcher's axe lying on top of it.

Knife in her dress pocket, she opened the door wide and spoke up. "Juliusz."

Juliusz sat up with a start, grabbed his axe, and turned around quickly, waving it around threateningly. When he saw her he cried, "Damn you, Tekla, you gave me a real fright." His evil smile bared crooked, yellow teeth. His eyes were bloodshot and glazed over, the expression in them was mad. "We killed those bastards," he chuckled.

Tekla's face turned to stone. "Who did?" she asked coolly.

Juliusz got up, tilting his head toward her. With an air of disparaging boastfulness, he stretched one leg in front of him and bowed like a knight, waving an invisible cap through the air. "Your humble servant," he said, then added, with the same breath, "now that you are free of these scoundrels, you can finally marry me."

Juliusz was five years older than her and a head shorter, with a strong, firm build. With his muscular arms, he easily hoisted calves twice his size onto his shoulder. Decent women rejected his clumsy advances, claiming that he reeked of beef guts. They weren't wrong. The smell of meat seemed to cling to him. But a man of great desires as Juliusz wasn't one to give up. Every evening after work he would go to the city baths and scrub his body for a long time before spritzing himself generously with French cologne and resuming his courting in vain. The women would take a whiff and exclaim, "Still stinks."

Quietly, Tekla said, "I don't think I'll marry you, Juliusz."

He shrugged indifferently. "You'll die an old maid, Tekla," he said, returning to the piles.

"We'll all die someday, Juliusz."

For years, he provided the rabbi's wife with chicken and beef. He was a devout Christian, and although the Goldsteins treated him fairly and extremely generously, he loathed them. But not only them. He hated all Yids. When the incited mob left the church and began to make its way toward the Jewish quarter, he rushed to the butcher shop as fast as his crooked legs could carry him, grabbed the axe from the wall, downed a bottle of liquor, and hurried back to join the others.

Tekla glanced askance at Daniel's bed. The bed was empty and the sheets were mussed, but no blood or signs of struggle were visible. She exhaled.

"Of course we'll all die someday," he chuckled, then added with a meaningful wink, "but you can live with me until you die."

"I'm much younger than you," she said sweetly. Then she teased, "Besides, I'm looking for a rich man. Really rich."

Malicious laughter rocked Juliusz's body. "You learned that from the Yids. Money, that's all you care about. Not heart, not soul. You're stupid, Tekla. You could have lived like a queen with me, but instead you chose to be a servant for the Yids. We can be rich if you just tell me where they hide their money."

She advanced toward him from behind, her hand in her pocket, holding onto the knife. "You know very well they have no money. You've let them run a tab. If memory serves, they still owe you."

He nodded. "They do, but we settled the debt today."

He bent down to search for an item that had fallen from his hands. This was her chance. Tekla raised the knife in both hands and landed it into his back as hard as she could. She felt his ribs breaking, his soft tissues tearing. Juliusz turned to face her, his face twisted with surprise and pain. His hand that was holding the axe rose and fell, and he collapsed onto his back.

"Damn Yid," he gargled, bloody foam bubbling over his mouth. "I should have killed you when I had the chance." Then he choked, blood jetting from his mouth, eyes rolling back in his head. "Save me," he grunted, then went still.

She quickly rummaged through a pile of clothes and pulled out a filthy jute sack, where Juliusz had tucked away the silver he'd pillaged. She picked up the sack and began to carefully search the other rooms. Daniel was nowhere.

She paused, at a loss. The racket outside grew louder. She had to find him quickly and get out of there. Suddenly, she recalled the woodshed, his favorite hiding place.

She found him tucked away between a wall and a woodpile, curled up in an old woolen blanket, fast asleep. She considered waking him, but she had to take care of Juliusz's body before the boy woke up. The thought of him witnessing the horror in the house gave her chills.

She locked the shed's door and walked back into the house, where she packed up her few belongings. Then she went down to the basement, picked up a tin of gasoline, and walked through the house, pouring the liquid through all the rooms. When she was finished, she struck a match.

Back in the woodshed, she carefully cut off Daniel's sideburns. She dropped the silky hair into a pouch, then woke the boy up tenderly.

Daniel opened two round, startled eyes. When he saw Tekla, he buried his head in her warm lap and went back to sleep.

Tekla waited until it was dark, then pulled Daniel onto her back and sneaked out, heading toward her aunt's house in a nearby village. The night was warm and bright. The smell of fresh grass from the harvested fields mixed with the smell of smoke from the burning houses. Faltering under her heavy load, she walked slowly, keeping pace, feet sinking into the soft dirt.

The flapping wings of wild geese, the distant bellowing of cattle, and the calling of night birds broke the silence. The world kept turning, screeching on its rusty axis. Only the Jews were gone.

She didn't permit him to play with the village kids. The presence of an unfamiliar boy could raise suspicions. Many people wouldn't hesitate to turn him in for a bag of wheat. These worries kept her up at night. Two weeks later, she decided to return to her home village, east of Bialystok. Before heading out, she placed a gold cross chain around Daniel's neck, and made him memorize his new name—Jozek.

From the years that followed, Goldstone remembered an old two-story stone house with a tall chimney and roosting storks. A gray stone wall flanked a spacious yard with fruit trees.

Tekla demolished the abandoned pigpen behind the house and built a chicken coop and a small doghouse instead, for the puppy she bought Daniel. Then she fixed the rest of the house, replacing the rotting pipes and the cracked roof tiles, polishing and waxing the floors.

Little Jozek was her entire world, and her happiness was complete. During their first nights in the village, he would wake up in a cold sweat, crying for his mother, his father, and his sisters. In the morning, he remembered nothing.

She traveled back to the city a year later. Almost

against her will, her feet led her to the Jewish quarter. While most of the other houses were now occupied by new residents, her employers' burnt-down house remained desolate. Signs pasted to the façade warned passersby against landslides and announced that the house was the property of the Polish government, and that any trespassers would be fined heftily.

At the neighborhood grocer's, Orzeszkowa was slicing a slab of sausage into fine strips, which she dropped onto greased paper with a flourish. Tekla greeted her, but the clerk went on the offensive without lingering on niceties.

"So, you're back, then?"

"No. Why would I be back?"

The clerk looked at her askance. "Have you heard of what happened to Juliusz?"

"I have. Such a terrible fate."

"Fate?" the woman chuckled. "Officer Kownacki said it was arson. If you ask me, it was murder."

Tekla tried to imbue her voice with genuine astonishment. "Murder? Are you certain?"

"I'm certain of nothing. What I'm saying is, there are rumors, and rumors have it that the same person who set the house on fire also stole the goods. Juliusz was inside, trapped in one of the bedrooms, suffocating to death. They didn't find even a single damn zloty around his body. Do you understand? It was all gone."

"But the family was poor. They had nothing."

The clerk glared at her. "I don't buy your stories. You truly think they'll find nothing? Not even the silver? Whoever killed him took it all. The officer told my

Zygmunt that nothing remained of that beast, Juliusz. Just an ash heap."

"So Juliusz killed the Goldsteins?"

The clerk's swift fingers paused in midair. It was a known secret that Juliusz coveted Tekla. Everyone had watched him woo her feverishly. At the pub, when he was intoxicated, he swore to all those present that he would be the man to deflower her. But when she rebuffed him time and time again, he began referring to her as Jewish swine.

The clerk sneered. "You knew him well, didn't you? You ought to know if he was capable of something like that."

"I don't know. One thing is for certain, Juliusz was handy with an axe."

"Nonsense," said the clerk. "That tells us nothing. Plenty of axes were raised that day. People used them to break down doors, locked closets, safety boxes. There were even some resistant Yids who took an axe blow to their heads. But not everyone murdered people. My Zygmunt, that weakling, only went in after the affair was already over. He brought home an old worm-gnawed bureau, and I was thinking what an idiot he was, was bringing me garbage again. But then—you aren't going to believe this—we found a trove of silver inside! I'm telling you—these Yids lived like paupers, but they were sitting on a treasure. You should have heard how they howled before they were butchered." The clerk knelt down to stack tin cans on the bottom shelves.

Her voice emerged from behind the counter. "And did you hear about their little boy?"

Tekla froze. "Heard about him? He was the first one I looked for when I arrived."

The clerk chuckled maliciously. "So, you wanted the little Yid all to yourself, did you?"

"The priest said we must rescue small souls. I wanted to baptize him."

The clerk slammed the tin cans one on top of another. "That old fool."

"The boy could have become a proper Christian."

The clerk got up from the floor and wiped her hands on her apron. "Baptized or not, his blood would remain Jewish. So? Did you find him?"

"No! I looked everywhere, but it was as if the earth had swallowed him."

The clerk put on her glasses, took the list from Tekla's hand, and began collecting the provisions. When she was finished, she tallied the bill. "You weren't the only one looking for him," she said. "About a month ago, his aunt and uncle came looking for him, all the way from America. They'd heard that one of the children had survived. The woman was tall and blond, like Greta Garbo, with a big hat and sunglasses. She kept complaining about the lousy weather.

"The man was fat, tall, his eyes filled with tears all the time. You should have heard his Polish. Not a hint of foreign accent. They wandered the streets for days, flashing pictures of the boy, questioning every person they met. They said they were willing to pay—in dollars!—for any piece of information. My Zygmunt searched the forest with his dog for three days straight, but found nothing. Only God knows where that boy is."

"He was never found?"

"No. The day before they took off, his fat uncle was standing in front of the burnt house, crying. The police told him they thought the boy had escaped to the woods, where someone must have killed and buried him, but officer Kownacki told us they'd found several bodies in the woods, but that none of them was a child."

Tekla counted the coins on the counter, took hold of her grocery basket, and turned to leave.

When she was already at the door, the clerk asked, "And what about you? Did you take nothing from the house?"

"Nothing. It was all on fire by the time I got there."

The clerk smirked and shrugged.

Passing by the burnt house, Tekla stopped on the street corner and wept voicelessly. She'd worked there for over twenty years and loved the Goldsteins as if they were her own kin. They'd never scolded her or raised their voices. With time, she became an expert on kosher laws and Shabbat traditions. She was fluent in Yiddish. Before leaving, she said a Hebrew blessing, crossed herself quickly, and rushed off to the train station.

In her home village, she introduced herself as the widow Tekla Maria Bodanowska, who was returning home with her young son, Jozek, following her husband's death. She lived on her grandmother Stefania

Sikorska's farm, the largest hog farm in the region. Stefania herself had buried three husbands in quick succession before dying all alone—not before leaving Tekla her abandoned homestead, including an enormous farmhouse with sooty walls and a wild, fecund garden.

Jozek attended the Carmelite sisters' monastery. Every morning, Tekla walked him to school and waved until he disappeared from view.

On Sundays, they'd walk together up the street leading to the church, moving slowly, his small hand in hers. In her wildest dreams, she'd never imagined such happiness was possible.

Jozek sang the Latin prayers fluently in the church's children's choir, his voice clear as a bell. At home, she spoke with him in Yiddish.

Tekla put off confession with Father Waszczykowski once and again. One Sunday, when he pointed her decisively toward the empty confessional, she shoved her large body inside as if coerced, then sat there in silence. Finally, the priest's reproachful cough liberated her tongue.

"Forgive me father, for I have sinned."

"Unburden yourself to the Lord, and you shall be relieved."

"I have sinned severely, an unforgivable sin."

"Your heart is pure, my child."

"I stole from my employers."

"That is a severe sin, but one that is reparable, my child, without a doubt."

"I stole something precious. Immeasurably valuable."

"Every theft is equally sinful. Our Lord does not attach meaning to monetary value. Is the item still in your possession?"

"It is, but my employers are now dead."

"In that case, the item is deposited with you. Return it to their successors and ask forgiveness."

"Their successors are dead too."

"Are there any distant relatives?"

"If there are, I do not know them."

"It is your duty to seek them out, and return the stolen goods to them."

For months, Father Waszczkowski had been watching Jozek from a distance, from the corner of his eye. The child had certainly been gifted with many great qualities: handsome, quick-witted, a good Christian with perfect pitch and the voice of a meadowlark.

One Sunday, after mass, the father walked Tekla to the door. "Pani Bodanowska," he said, "you must have already guessed that your son has a bright future ahead of him."

Tekla shivered. "I wish I could afford to pay for pipe organ lessons for him with Ms. Szymborska, but—"

"I'm not referring to music, Pani Bodanowska. I'm referring to priesthood."

Tekla's mouth fell open. "Priesthood? I thought this was about his talent for..."

The priest waved the thought away. "His musical talent is a gratis gift. The voice of any child, as dulcet as it might be, inevitably changes. On rare occasions, it improves, but more often than not it is discovered to be merely average. We are talking here about something far superior."

"We?"

"Bishop Dombrowski is also involved."

"Bishop Dombrowski?"

Father Waszczykowski rebuked her with his eyes.

"His Holiness Bishop Dombrowski is your region's cardinal, Pani Bodanowska."

"Of course."

The offer was generous. The boy would attend a theologian seminary in Krakow, where he would study alongside the sons of bishops, clerics, and other members of the highest echelons.

Meekly, she said, "Forgive me, Father, but I don't think I could withstand it."

"Is this about money?" he scolded. "Pani, please don't concern yourself with that. When it comes to matters of spirituality, money is meaningless. Our bishop has a fabulous relationship with Father Wladyslaw Milosz, the head of the seminary. The boy will receive a full scholarship that would free you from having to worry about his livelihood for the rest of his days. He will receive the finest education and people will kiss the ends of his robe. What could be better?"

Tekla froze.

The priest waited impatiently, his foot tapping the floor nervously.

"He's too young," she finally murmured. "He still needs me. He's the only thing I have in this world."

The father held back his anger. "You must stop thinking only about yourself, Pani Bodanowska. A good Christian doesn't think about herself, especially not when the future of a brilliant child is on the line. This boy is a gift from God, and you must treat him as such."

Tekla flushed. "The boy is sick," she whispered, crossing herself. "He is ill with the same disease that took his father from us."

"My goodness."

"He requires my constant supervision."

The priest raised a curious eyebrow. The child appeared perfectly healthy to him, practically bursting with vitality. "Then we shall wait until he recovers."

As she descended the stairs outside of the church, he called after her, "Your son has been baptized, has he not?"

She turned back slowly. "Of course. My Jozek is a good Christian."

Father Waszczykowski furrowed his brow. "It's a conundrum," he said. "When I sent the Bialystok Archive a request for a copy of his baptism certificate, I was informed that no such record existed."

"He wasn't baptized in Bialystok. My late husband's parents insisted that we have the ceremony in Jedwabne, in the same church where his father had been baptized. That church was burnt to the ground during the war. The archive is completely gone."

One evening in late October, a loud knock came at the door.

Tekla looked through the peephole. On the doorstep, she saw a middle-aged man in a dark suit and a young woman with blond hair, wearing sunglasses. They were accompanied by a local uniformed police officer.

Tekla held her breath, praying for them to leave, but these people were determined. The cop knocked again, louder this time.

Tekla opened the door. Graciously, she asked how she could help them.

The young woman said softly that they were there on the matter of Daniel Goldstein. She asked if they could come in and ask her a few questions.

Tekla eyed them suspiciously. "Who are you?"

The woman removed her sunglasses. "We're here on behalf of Rabbi Goldstein's relatives to find his son, Daniel. We received a reliable tip that he survived the pogrom." Her Polish was flawless.

"I don't know you," said Tekla. Just as she was about to slam the door, the man in a suit wedged his foot in the door.

Coldly, the police officer asked, "Is your name Tekla Bodanowska?"

"Yes."

"The police are investigating the disappearance of a child. If you don't cooperate, I'll have no choice but to take you into the station for an interrogation. Is that clear?"

Tekla nodded, frightened.

"Before the war, did you work on Steppe Street, in the home of the late Rabbi Isar Alter Goldstein?"

"I did."

"How many years did you work there?"

"I can't remember. Ever since I was a girl."

"Do you know what became of them?"

"They were all murdered."

"All of them?"

"I saw their bodies with my own eyes."

"Did you see the body of the little boy?"

"He died in the woods," Tekla cried. "Officer Kownacki said he is buried in the woods."

"But you haven't seen his body with your own eyes."

"The officer said many bodies were found in the woods."

"How could Officer Kownacki identify Daniel's body if he'd never met him?" the cop asked.

Trapped, panicked, she stuttered, "I don't know. I'm only telling you what I heard from the grocer."

The young woman touched her arm gently. "We need to talk. We'd better sit down."

They led her into the kitchen, where they sat her down and gave her a glass of water. "Drink up," they said. "You need to calm down."

Her throat was clogged. Water dribbled from the corners of her mouth.

Her world had been turned upside down. She cried voicelessly, clawing at her thighs. The young woman sat down beside her and placed a comforting hand on Tekla's arm. She told her that the American relatives remembered her fondly.

When they'd discovered that the boy's name was missing from the police's list of casualties, they came looking for him, in vain. The neighbors wouldn't tell them anything. After that, they hired a former police investigator from a nearby town. The man leased an apartment in town and assumed the identity of a retired teacher. He had a generous, amiable personality. He spent evenings at the local pub, smoking and playing cards. He often treated the other patrons to a round of drinks.

When pub-goers began to feel comfortable around him, they let their tongues loose. Everyone knew about the Christian nanny who was versed in Jewish law. In a matter of weeks, he discovered the name of the village where she now resided. One morning, he showed up at the local post office and introduced himself as a messenger tasked with personally delivering a package sent from abroad. The postal worker suspected nothing, and gave him the address without hesitation.

"Please understand," the young woman now told Tekla, "the child must be brought to his relatives. They are destroyed by this family tragedy."

Tekla broke into wails, slapping her face with her hands. "My child!" she cried in Polish, then mumbled in Yiddish, "*Mein kind! Kein einer wat nemen mein kind!*"

"*Zant ir Yiddish?*" the woman asked.

"No!" Tekla howled. "No!" Then, in Polish, she said, "I've raised this child from the day he was born. He knows me. Only me."

"Do you know Isak?" asked the man.

Tekla looked at him dully. "Isak?"

"The boy's uncle. The Warsaw merchant."

"Iche," said Tekla. "His name is Iche."

"Yes, of course," said the man. "Iche."

"Iche doesn't even know the boy," Tekla said contemptuously. "He didn't even attend his *bris*. But if Iche takes Jozek to Warsaw, I'll go with him. I'll live with Jozek in Warsaw."

The man in the suit said, "Isak doesn't live in Warsaw anymore. He lives in America now. We'll take him to Palestine first, and Isak will come take him to America from there."

"America? Palestine?" Tekla rolled the words incredulously in her mouth. America and Palestine were foreign planets, light years away from her world. Pleadingly, she turned to the officer and took hold of his arms. "Officer, they can't just take my child away. I raised him, I risked my life for him. They can't do it. You can't let them do that to me. There are laws, you can't just do something like that to a person."

The officer shook her hands off. "The boy is a Yid," he said. "Besides, they've got a court order."

She froze. Jozek, eyes blurry with sleep, was standing at the top of the stairs, barefoot. He looked down through heavy eyelids, and when he noticed Tekla's pained face he rushed to her, falling into her open arms.

Tekla bellowed in heartrending animalistic grief, then let out a yell, and fainted.

The man pulled a syringe from his doctor's bag and injected her with a tranquilizer. Then he carried the child back to bed.

The visitors remained in her home for a week. They told Jozek stories about his family in America. He was charmed by the color photographs. Here were his cousins riding ponies; there they were rowing a boat in the lake outside of their house; and there, at Shabbat dinner, wearing blue silk yarmulkes around a table with burning candles and two braided challahs. They spoke the foreign names to him: Laura, Jimmy, Aunt Hillary. Jozek repeated the names, mesmerized.

Pale and puffy eyed, Tekla wandered the rooms like a ghost, crying and mumbling unintelligibly to herself.

Once, the young woman tried to comfort her. Eyes burning with madness, Tekla cried, "I'm Jewish! I'm Jewish! Rabbi Isar said I have the soul of a Jew, that my soul received the Torah on Mount Sinai. Look!" She pulled a book off the shelf with trembling fingers. "Here," she told the young woman. "Ein Jacob, read it. You're Jewish. Read it and explain what you just said."

The young woman glanced at the book. "I can't read Hebrew," she said.

"I can," Tekla declared defiantly. "The rabbi taught me. I can understand it all. I read the Mishna and Psalms. I say the blessings, perform the dough offering ceremony, and say the Shema prayer with Jozek in bed at night. 'The angel who delivered me from all harm.'

What must a woman do to be officially Jewish? Take a dip in the *mikveh*? I can do that."

The young woman's eyes welled up. "But the child needs his family," she said tenderly. "And they need him too. He's their only survivor."

Tekla slapped her own chest violently. "He's the only one I have left, too. I've got nobody in this world but him!" she cried. "I'm his family, I'm the one who saved him from those murderers, I'm the one who carried him in my arms all day long while his uncle was safe and comfortable in America."

"You know his uncle never stopped looking for him."

Tekla buried her tearful face in her red hands. "I won't interfere," she sobbed. "I'll live nearby. I'll keep watch from afar. He won't notice a thing. It won't bother them. I'll be around just in case."

"He'll be in good hands, Tekla," said the young woman. "You can stay in touch with him. We'll make sure of that, I promise you."

Tekla spent their last night together sitting beside the boy's bed, drilling her eyes into him, committing every gesture and facial tic to memory. When he asked her, through half-open lids, why she was crying, she told him they were tears of joy and quickly wiped them away.

"I'm glad for you," she said, voice broken. "You'll be happy there. You'll meet your family and play with your cousins. You can sail in the lake and ride ponies."

His eyes pierced her. All of a sudden, he sat up and wrapped his arms around her waist.

Tekla dropped her head against his shoulders and cried. "Don't forget Tekla. Don't forget poor old Tekla who loves you so."

The next morning, she stood at the gate in her good dress, hair braided, and eyes puffy. She wanted him to remember her at her best. When she asked to accompany him to the seaport, his new caretakers politely declined.

"There's no point in that, Tekla. He should remember you in the home he loved, not some strange place like the port."

She stayed beside the gate, weeping and waving goodbye. When the car finally disappeared around the bend, she collapsed to the ground.

They corresponded for the first few years. Then they had long weekly phone calls. Six years after he left, she wrote to tell him she'd married Stanislaw the greengrocer—a jolly, generous widower who alleviated her loneliness. Occasionally she sent Daniel sweaters and hats made of the finest yarn she could find. She made them oversized, so that they may warm him for years to come. They carried the faraway scent of lavender, so familiar that it brought tears to his eyes whenever he wore them.

Later, when he became a successful lawyer, he sent her a sizeable sum of money each month. When she fell ill, he begged her to come live with him in America.

"Come to me," he told her over the phone. "Bring your old man. I'll take care of both of you."

Tekla said no. Her husband was too sick to withstand the rough road. So was she. "You must live your life," she replied. "I don't want to be a burden."

That year, when he attended an international conference in Warsaw as the representative of the New York Attorney General, he decided to drop by for a surprise visit. A month earlier, when they spoke on the phone, she sounded very sick and weak. Her husband had recently passed away, and she was now on her own.

Goldstone rented a car and drove to Bialystok, where he wandered the downtown shops and bought her everything he could think of: fine sausages, bathrobes, towels, housewares, and a gold chain bearing his name. He loaded it all into his rental car and drove off to the village.

When he got off the highway and onto the familiar dirt road, the old aromas invaded his nostrils. Everything was just as he'd remembered it: the forests, the bare red tree trunks, the scorched fallow fields, the dirt battery on the shore of the lake, the swans floating horizontally across it, as light as Japanese origami.

He parked the car in the old market plaza, and walked across a wooden bridge over the river, breathing in the moldy smell of rotting leaves. In the shimmering water beneath him, he saw the tired reflection of a man in his late thirties, his cheeks sunken and his hair graying at the temples.

On Smocza Street, he walked into the pub for a glass of Wyborowa. A group of middle-aged men were playing cards and smoking. They glanced at him indifferently before returning to their affairs. Goldstone downed a glass and walked back out, the liquid burning through him, leaving a pleasant warmth in its wake.

He arrived at the house at dusk. The old gas lamps on the street had been replaced with electric lights. At the small public garden, he turned onto a narrow path leading to the house, carrying the packages in his arms. The lights were on inside. The broken iron gate was tilted. All over the yard were toys and colorful plastic balls.

He knocked hesitantly. He heard a baby crying and a woman shushing. A masculine voice spoke farther away. He waited a moment, and just as he raised his hand to knock again the door swung open.

A young woman in a filthy house robe, her hair in a messy bun, a bawling baby in her arms, was standing before him, fixing him with languidly suspicious eyes. She shifted her gaze back into the house and called out a man's name.

Hesitating, Goldstone asked, "Excuse me, but is Pani Bodanowska here? Tekla?

"She doesn't live here anymore," the woman barked.

"What do you mean?"

A man appeared behind the woman and looked Daniel over suspiciously. In the meek light of the hallway lamp, he practically looked like a boy. He had large, crooked adolescent teeth, a heavy jaw, and blue eyes. Two days' worth of stubble adorned his otherwise smooth face.

"She already told you," the man said resolutely, "she doesn't live here anymore."

"Where does she live now?"

There was a momentary silence as the couple exchanged looks. Even the baby piped down, his eyes tracking the wordless dialogue with curiosity. Suddenly, he dropped his weight toward the shiny bags and cellophane paper in Daniel's hands. The girl lost her balance and pulled him toward her violently. The baby screamed.

Mockingly, the boy said, "She lives on the edge of the village. Beyond the fence."

"What?"

The girl glared at her husband. "She died," she chastised. Then, testing Daniel's reaction, she added, "about a month ago."

"Died?"

The man laughed maliciously. "Yes. Dead, finished. Exactly a month ago. Sepsis. Long story short, she lost consciousness and was dead within two weeks. But don't look so worried, the doctors said she didn't suffer too much."

Eyes narrowed, the woman asked, "What is your relationship with her?"

Goldstone hesitated. The man's suspicious eyes were stalking him. "Her nephew."

The man whistled with disbelief. "Her nephew? And you didn't know she was sick? Didn't hear she'd died? You only care about her after she's already gone, huh?."

"I came to visit her. I live in America. We've kept in touch. Regular phone calls. When she stopped calling I came right over." He shook the bags in his hands, as if to prove the purity of his intentions. The baby giggled with pleasure. "And what are you to her?"

The man opened his eyes to curse at him, but Goldstone beat him to the punch.

"You're Stanislaw's son, aren't you? Her husband's son?"

The woman intervened. "No, I'm Stanislaw's daughter." Then, quickly, she added, "Tekla left the house to me."

Goldstone smiled. The banal, pathetic simplicity of the couple thrilled and disgusted him in equal measures. They were dirt poor, defending their new lair with bare teeth. When it came to their house, they were prepared to rip him to shreds. He placed the bags on the floor. "These are for you," he said.

The man took Goldstone's hand in his rough palms. An ingratiating, grateful smile revealed his bad teeth again. The danger had passed. Goldstone pulled his hand away and walked off.

When he was already at the gate, the girl called after him. "Wait!"

She ran over, carrying a small package wrapped in brown paper. "She never mentioned a nephew, even when she was very sick. You'd think she would have said—"

Goldstone cut her off. "I was more than a nephew to her. She never mentioned someone named Daniel?"

The girl considered this for a moment, then shook her head. "Not that I recall."

"Wait a minute! Jozek! Did she ever mention a Jozek?"

The woman's eyes widened. From the window, the man urged her to come back inside. "She did speak about Jozek. Many times. Many, many times, but only at the very end. I thought it must have been her son who died as a child, but I couldn't ask her at that point. She wasn't all there anymore. Is that you? Are you her son?"

"No. Well, yes. Something like that."

Inside, the baby was screaming. The man lost patience and shouted at her from the window.

She pushed the package into his hands. "I've got to get back. I think this belongs to you."

Goldstone tore the paper with trembling hands. Inside the package were the clothes he'd worn on the horrible day of the pogrom. Four ends of his tallit were now resting in his hands, carefully folded, along with a yarmulke and his shorn sideburns.

He buried his face in the clothes and wept.

Justice John Paul Roberts suggested that Goldstone run his cross-examination from his seat behind the prosecution's desk. In response, Goldstone drew his head back, grabbed the wooden armrests with the tips of his fingers, and propelled his body upwards. He stood in place for a moment, swaying from side to side. When he tried to approach the stand, his knees buckled and he collapsed with a thump at the foot of the defendant, who watched him expressionlessly, without a hint of gloating. "Like a bag of bones," he told his children later. "A ratty leather bag of dried bones."

He was only unconscious for a minute or two. When he awoke, his field of vision was filled with the gorgeous face of the court stenographer. The white collar of her dress emphasized the warm, rich darkness of her skin. For a moment, he thought he might be dead. He expected to hear the holy spirit in her deep voice, that heavenly Jewish entity of eternal kindness which welcomes the souls of the dead at the edge of a dark tunnel, leading them to Jewish heaven, surrounded by clouds of confetti, *mitzvahs*, and good deeds.

His delusions were cut short.

The court's superintendent, a flushed Irish man with enormous arms, pulled him up from the floor and sat him down in his chair. Then he handed him a glass of water. Goldstone's hands trembled, the water spilling and leaving a round, shameful stain on his crotch.

But that wasn't the end of his mortification. In the chaos that ensued, someone urgently called for a doctor. Then, in an act of diabolical humiliation, the defendant quickly descended from the stand, kneeled before a stunned Goldstone, and moved his finger back and forth before his face, instructing Goldstone to follow it with his eyes. Then he felt the man's skull, limbs, and ribs. Finally, he addressed the judge.

"Everything is fine, sir," he said matter-of-factly. "No broken bones, no head injury. Only bruises. He'll live."

The judge's gray fish eyes looked over Goldstone with concern. The prosecutor's face was pale, his hands shaking with weakness. The judge angled a questioning look at the defense. Stunned, Blumenthal confirmed his agreement with a nod. The judge announced that the next session would be postponed until after the holiday break.

The results of his medical tests were satisfactory. Goldstone was found capable of performing his duties. His diagnosis included exhaustion, low blood pressure, and—more than anything— stress.

His sons hurried to his apartment. His dramatic collapse was shown on the news every hour. Their father's dazed face, twisted with pain, also appeared in every evening paper.

They scolded their father for his stubbornness. "Why did you insist on standing? It could have cost you your life. What good would you be to anybody if you broke your neck?"

Then they informed him that, until the trial was over, one of them would always be staying with him.

Goldstone turned them down. "No need for that. Tony is here. When I decide it's time to die, I'll give you advance notice."

But this time, they would not back off. "We'll come by every night to make sure you're okay."

At the next session, Goldstone questioned Dr. von Antrim from a seated position. "What is your religious affiliation? Jewish? Christian?"

"I don't subscribe to any specific religion."

"What is your religious identity?"

"I was brought up Jewish from a young age."

"What was your parents' faith?"

"My father was baptized as a Protestant, though he was a self-defined atheist. My mother was raised Christian. Her father and grandfather were Protestants."

"In your deposition dated December 4th, you stated that your mother belonged to the Jewish faith."

"That's true. But later, at a medical conference in London, I found out that my mother did not, in fact, have any Jewish heritage."

"Prior to that, were you in possession of any documents confirming your mother's Jewish identity?"

"Beyond a letter from the Gestapo claiming that my mother was Jewish, we had no other documents confirming her Judaism."

"Meaning, that based on a letter from the Gestapo,

you chose to introduce yourself to Jewish survivors as a Jewish man."

"At the time I had no doubt that was the truth."

"You also spoke about the Jewish education you received, about observing the Shabbat as a child, attending synagogue..."

"I believed I was, indeed, Jewish, and said as much."

"It was misrepresentation."

"It was fact."

"When did you begin to fertilize these Jewish women with your own semen? Didn't you think there was a problem here? You being German, and all?"

"In the waiver, the plaintiff did not mention any issues with using a German donor."

"Wouldn't that be obvious? At least when it came to Jewish survivors of Nazi extermination camps?"

"Not to me."

Goldstone raised his voice. "Was your father not a Nazi war criminal who was executed after having sent hundreds of thousands of Jews to their deaths?"

"Objection, your honor," Blumenthal interjected. "The prosecution is attempting, time and again, to accuse my client for the sins of his father. I ask that the question be struck from the protocol. In addition, I'd ask that the prosecutor cease and desist promptly."

"Sustained."

Goldstone took a long sip from his water. The pain pricking his waist and the numbing in his feet had renewed. He swallowed a painkiller and closed his eyes. When the justice asked if he needed to take a break, he said no, then turned back to William.

"As a specialist, were you aware of the medical risks involved in in-vitro fertilization?"

"Of course."

"When I say medical risks, I'm referring to congenital birth defects and a variety of genetic conditions."

"All risks were considered. We retained the services of Professor Katrina Hedwig Mayer, a genetics specialist of international renown."

"Are your donors required to sign a medical confidentiality waiver?"

"Of course. That is required by law."

"What is included?"

"Donors are obligated to report hereditary conditions, mental illness in the family, financial state, personal status, etc."

"Did you turn some potential donors away based on these self reports?"

"Only when it came to severe conditions."

Goldstone lingered. "Such as?"

William hesitated. "Mostly conditions such as cancer, mental retardation, autism, and psychiatric illness."

"If a donor is discovered to have one of these conditions after the fertilization, would you continue the pregnancy or terminate it at once?"

"We would recommend termination."

"Even if the mother wished to continue?"

"We have no legal authority to force the mother to abort the pregnancy."

"Are the criteria for Jewish patients different than the ones defined for other women?"

"Certainly. Jewish refugees who underwent terrible tragedy have a limited capacity for raising children with disabilities."

"Then one might say that you and Professor Mayer decided which women would be fertilized and with which donation?"

"I suppose every fertilization specialist has to make these decisions."

"I was asking about your patients."

"Then the answer is yes."

Goldstone pierced the defendant with a withering gaze. "In other words," he said, "you might say that a pair of German doctors with Nazi backgrounds decided for survivors of the extermination camps which children would be joining the Jewish people and which would not."

"Your honor," Blumenthal burst out, "I won't stand for this. The prosecution is attempting to determine my client's fate on account of his father's past. I demand that this question be stricken and that the jury be instructed to discount it."

The judge pounded the gavel. "Sustained." Then, with anger in his voice, he turned to Goldstone. "I'm warning you, one more comment like that and I will be forced to terminate your examination."

Goldstone rose slowly from his seat and limped over to the witness stand on his cane. "In your estimation, how many of the thousands of Jewish women you fertilized with your own sperm could have afforded this sort of treatment without your help?"

Blumenthal stood up. "Objection, your honor, my client is not a statistician. Besides, we are not in possession of the necessary data to answer that question."

"Your honor, the prosecution desires a rough estimate in order to prove manipulation of patients on the part of the defendant."

"Overruled. Please repeat the question."

"Roughly, please state what percentage of these women could have afforded to pay in full for fertilization treatments and the close medical care you provided."

"I don't know. A small percentage, most likely."

"A number?"

"I'd say about ten percent."

"Only ten percent. Meaning, the vast majority of these women had no other recourse."

"They were still free to choose any other clinic."

"Theoretically, yes. But in practice, without private medical insurance or financial ability, they would have had to give up on their dream of bearing a child."

"Subsidized health insurance programs also offer fertility treatments."

"Is it true that these programs only offer free fertility treatments to American citizens?"

"That's correct."

"And how many of your patients are American citizens?"

"Only a few of them."

"Going by your experience, how many fertility treatments on average are required in order to bring a baby into the world?"

"That varies. To answer that, one must take many factors into account, such as age of the patient, physical and mental health."

"On average."

"On average it takes two to three rounds of IVF, though sometimes more."

"In other words, a Jewish refugee who is not an American citizen and does not have private medical insurance cannot afford fertility treatments."

"Most likely not."

"Did you provide most of the sperm donations?"

"Once I found out I wasn't actually Jewish, I became the main donor."

"Why you?"

"For convenience's sake."

"Meaning, you viewed yourself as a quality donor, to use your clinic's lingo."

"Correct."

"Who would you define as the ideal donor?"

"I wouldn't use the term 'ideal.' But generally speaking, a quality donor is defined as an intelligent person of able mind and body, with good genes and an attractive appearance."

"What do you mean by good genes?"

"Without a family history of severe hereditary diseases."

"Meaning that after consulting with genetics specialist Katrina Mayer, the two of you decided unanimously that you are the worthiest candidate for fertilizing thousands of Jewish patients who survived death at Auschwitz, Birkenau, Dachau, and Bergen-Belsen."

William met Goldstone's eyes. "I've never claimed to be the worthiest candidate," he said softly, "but I'm certainly suitable."

Goldstone rifled through his papers for a long moment. "Would you tell me please," he said, "if the names Peter and Heinrich von Antrim mean anything to you?"

"Of course. They are my paternal cousins."

"Is it true that both of them are severely mentally retarded?"

Blumenthal raised his hand. "Objection, your honor. My client's cousins' mental state has nothing to do with this lawsuit."

"Your honor," Goldstone barked, "the prosecution is taking steps to prove that the defendant's medical conduct was in complete opposition to the criteria he himself had defined, not to mention in opposition to the rules of ethics, especially when considering his patients' difficult backgrounds."

"Objection overruled, the witness will answer the question."

Dr. von Antrim flushed. "Their retardation is not genetic," he said measuredly. "Peter and Heinrich were born in a complicated caesarean and suffered lack of oxygen flow to the brain for an extended period of time. Their mother died during childbirth."

Goldstone limped closer. "And your uncle Hans, their father?" he asked. "Isn't it true that your uncle was in and out of psychiatric hospitals throughout his life?"

"My uncle was a very sensitive man. The war led him to suffer a severe nervous breakdown from which he never recovered."

Goldstone smiled with derision. "Was it sending his old cello professor to the crematorium that shook him so badly?"

Blumenthal raised his hand. "Your honor," he called, "I ask that this line of questioning be dropped."

Goldstone turned to the judge. "Your honor, yesterday the prosecution obtained documents confirming that Hans suffered from paranoid schizophrenia. His two sons were retarded. There is a high prevalence of mental illness in his close family. Nevertheless, the defendant—allegedly in consultation with a renowned geneticist, decided that he was a suitable donor, and used his own sperm in order to impregnate Jewish refugees."

"Carry on."

Goldstone moved closer to the defendant, determined. "To the best of your professional knowledge, is mental illness hereditary?"

"I'm not an expert, but there are studies that point to a genetic component in certain mental illnesses, yes."

"Meaning that we might conclude that if a person suffers of mental illness, their offspring would suffer the same?"

"To the best of my knowledge, yes."

"And would it be reasonable to say that a murderer suffers from severe mental illness?"

"That is certainly possible."

Goldstone grabbed the sides of the stand and glared at the man. "Dr. von Antrim," he asked, "are you aware of the war crimes your father committed?"

Blumenthal jumped up from his seat. "Objection, your honor. My client's father's past, whatever it may be, has nothing to do with the subject of this lawsuit."

The judge turned to Goldstone. "I hope you have a weighty argument for carrying on with this line of questioning."

Goldstone nodded. "The defendant has admitted that murderers suffer some form of mental illness, and that these illnesses have a genetic component. Therefore, we can reasonably conclude that the defendant passed on his mentally ill father's genes to the plaintiff's child."

"Your honor, the prosecution is making sweeping, unfounded generalizations—"

"Overruled. Mr. Goldstone, please complete this line of questioning quickly and avoid generalizations. Now please repeat your question for the court minutes."

Goldstone turned to William. "Once more, are you aware that your father committed war crimes?"

"I have no proof of this."

Goldstone looked through his papers. Without raising his head, he asked, "Are you claiming you know nothing about your father's past?"

"A few years ago I learned that he had been the commander of a border crossing camp in Ukraine. I was told he was charged with the orderly passage of Jews from Eastern European countries into Poland."

"You mean to say that your father was in charge of death transports to extermination camps in Poland—

camps such as Treblinka, Auschwitz, Birkenau, Majdanek, and Sobibor?"

"Yes."

Goldstone placed a photograph on the witness stand. "Does this image look familiar? Do you recognize the man in uniform on the right?"

"I do."

"Where do you know him from?"

"He's my father."

"Have you seen this photo before?"

"I received it at a medical conference in London from a gynecologist who claimed he'd served with my father during the war."

"Do you recognize the man beside him?"

"I do."

"Would you tell us who he is?"

"That's the man I met."

"And what can be seen in the background?"

William swallowed. "Ten hanging victims."

"Jewish?"

"I can't say that for sure."

"Do you know where this picture was taken?"

"As far as I know, it was taken in Treblinka."

"That's correct. And did you know that 870,000 people were murdered in Treblinka, 99.5% of them Jewish?"

"In that case, the people in the photo are likely Jewish."

"Then, knowing that your father was in charge of shipments of Jews to Auschwitz, Treblinka, Majdanek, Birkenau, and Sobibor, means your father was fully complicit in the murder of hundreds of thousands of Jews. Do you know if your father suffered of any kind of mental illness or mental disorder?"

"Not to the best of my knowledge."

"As a doctor, do you believe he suffered from mental illness or mental disorder?"

Blumenthal roared, "Objection, your honor! Apart from the fact that the defendant is not a psychiatrist, he did not know his father. I call to end this line of questioning."

Goldstone raised his hands. "Your honor, the prosecution rests."

Blumenthal stood up. "Just one question," he said, shifting his eyes to the jury. "Would you please tell the court why a reputable doctor like yourself, with a thriving practice, spends millions of his own capital for the purpose of fertilizing barren Jewish women?"

William closed his eyes. "It's the least I could do for them."

"No further questions, your honor."

Katrina Maria Hedwig Mayer, international molecular genetics specialist, lost her husband unexpectedly. He suffered a lethal heart attack in the middle of a very vigorous, very intimate moment. Herman Hedwig collapsed onto the floor of his Tübingen cottage. It was instant. A peaceful smile was on his face as his heart took its final beat. The girl he'd spent the night with was completely hysterical. She pushed the limp body off her with terror, and proceeded to run amok around the room, buck naked, screaming like a banshee.

Katrina arrived first. Her cool demeanor with the girl was inspiring. First, she wrapped one of her expensive Chinese silk robes around the girl's body, and then she sent her home before the place turned into a scene. Next, she sat beside the bed, took a long swig of neat whiskey, and watched the deceased's pink face gradually turn waxy, a sneaky expression of pleasure congealing over it.

She'd never known that kind of desire in her life. With a hint of envy, she thought this was a worthy death for any person, and certainly for an eighty-seven-year-old man like her husband. There were no agonies of old age, no pain. It ended with a groan or two, and with unadulterated lust.

The good people of the municipal funeral home arrived quickly, formal to the tips of their polished shoes. They wore black frocks and top hats, silver pins on their lapels. Though they may have enjoyed a private chuckle at the amusing sight, they did their jobs with respectful stoicism. They placed the dead man on his back in bed, limbs spread apart. His grotesquely hardened genitals continued to protrude from underneath the sheet while his arms were folded across his chest. His face beamed with the purest joy, seen only in the paintings of Christian martyrs whose beatific suffering was distilled into ecstatic pleasure.

The staff members from the funeral home were satisfied. The deceased, who had prepared himself carefully for the act of lovemaking, was clean, perfumed, and showered. All they had to do was straighten things out, put him in his finest suit, lightly powder the wizened cheeks, slip a red carnation into his lapel, and place him in a mahogany casket lined with crimson velvet.

Though they'd lived apart for years, Katrina and Herman remained close friends. At his elegant funeral, she gave him an emotional eulogy. The tears that streamed down her face during the reading of the will at the notary's office were also genuine. Though Herman left most of his fortune to his only nephew, he left his share of the steel conglomerate exclusively to her.

Katrina chanced upon the feature article about William's philanthropic project in *Frankfurter Allgemeine Zeitung* and was thrilled. They'd fallen out of touch again, having revived their connection at his grandmother's funeral. She resented him, disappointed when he did not return to his grandmother's abandoned mansion upon receiving his share of the inheritance, in order to restore it to its glory days. She gave different excuses to reject his invitations to come visit him in America.

Now, she decided she'd contribute to his project, in the form of her thriving agricultural fertilizer factory in Stuttgart, and she devoted the earnings to whatever purpose William saw fit to use them. In the letter she wrote him, she asked if she could come for a brief visit to America in order to transfer factory ownership and get a better idea of his project.

Katrina sounded nervous on the phone, her deep alto rich with emotion.

When he thanked her for her contribution and invited her for a long visit to New York, he heard her stifling a cry of excitement. Then, in a hollow voice, she said she didn't want to be a burden.

At Newark Airport, he spotted her waiting by the gates in a gray suit and black heels. Her right hand resting on an enormous suitcase, she carefully surveyed the crowd. She'd lost a lot of weight since the funeral. Her features had sharpened, rendering her face more aggressive. Her blond hair was pulled into a tight bun, and the once broad body had grown bony. Only her hips remained wide and pear-shaped.

When he called her name, she whipped her head toward him, then froze for a moment before breaking into a faltering, high-heeled run in his direction.

At the coffee shop in the gas station near the airport, she told him what he already knew. There were no dark secrets to be uncovered, nor malicious intent. What he found instead was a deep well of sadness and dark reserves of existential lonesomeness. William listened to her with shimmering eyes, indulging in the southern German dialect of his childhood.

When they got back on the highway, she asked that he take her to the hotel. "I'm exhausted. That flight killed me."

When he told her she'd be staying with him, she protested meekly. "I don't want to be a burden."

"Nonsense. I live all alone in an enormous apartment. You'll have an entire wing all to yourself."

She smiled with tired satisfaction. "How's your mother?"

"Fantastic. Last year she married a famous journalist and moved with him to San Francisco. She's sixty-five years old and her husband is almost a decade younger. You should have seen how she glowed on her wedding day. She looked much younger than her age."

Katrina's eyes clouded over. Her efforts to look her best and be liked by him suddenly seemed pathetic. "Your mother was always a beautiful woman," she said, giving in. "I'd love to see her."

William said nothing. He doubted his mother would agree to see Katrina. She'd fumed at Katrina's complete estrangement during the many years they'd spent in America. "I don't imagine she'll come to New York. She's on her honeymoon in Florida and will only get back here in September."

"I'm not sure I'll still be here."

William glanced at her. "Who knows?" he smiled. "At any rate, I'm very happy you're here now."

His estate managers in Germany had conducted thorough research. They informed him that Katrina had transferred some steel factories to a Swiss holding company on a long-term contract, and that two months after her husband passed away, she resigned from the university and announced her retirement from academia. Renting out her house in Frankfurt and opening New York bank accounts attested to an intention to settle down in America, they wrote to him.

Two months into her arrival, Katrina had become immersed in the life of the city's small German community. While William worked at the clinic into the small hours of the night, Katrina and her new friends went out to restaurants, Broadway shows, SoHo gallery openings, and concerts at Carnegie Hall.

"I'm happy," she confessed to him one night over dinner. "New York is the place for me."

She appeared recovered, brimming with vitality and plans for the future. Over time, she'd adopted some American mannerisms. Her gray, conservative European garb was replaced with colorful, tight-fitting clothes. Her tight blond coif was now a chestnut mane of curls.

William smiled. "I'm glad you're here."

Two weeks later, when she told William that, following a fervent search, she planned to buy an apartment in his building, he pretended to be surprised.

"Buy an apartment? Aren't you comfortable here?"

"I'm very comfortable, but I want my own place. I'm here to stay, at least for a few years. If you'd rather I didn't live in your building, just tell me. I haven't signed anything yet."

"Why would I not want that?"

Katrina smiled cunningly. "I suppose you already knew about it."

William saw no point in denying the allegations. "Yes," he said, "I've known about your intentions for a long time."

She fell silent, hesitating. Finally, without meeting his eyes, she quickly said, "Look, William, at first I was very upset with you for abandoning us, especially after you'd inherited everything. We all expected you to come back and be with us, to build your life near us. It was Grandma's dream. She so wanted to see small children running around the mansion. But today I understand your need to get away from that house, from Germany. The place is steeped in bad memories. I also want a change. I want to be part of your project. You know I have the know-how and the experience. I can help."

William said, "I'm treating extermination camp survivors."

"I know."

"These women have been through hell. Besides severe physical problems, they also have plenty of psychological trauma."

"I can imagine."

"Not many people last in this field."

"I thought I could help with medical testing and the ongoing management of the clinic. I've got plenty of experience."

The pictures the women showed Katrina were torn or crumpled. The people in them were yellowed with tears and stained with blood and kisses. In them, Katrina saw the faces of the murdered—parents, husbands, siblings, children. The women wanted to have babies in their images. Scared to death of the thought that their babies' faces might don the features of the dead, they asked her to pick their donor.

Katrina was surprised. "You want me to choose?"

"Yes, you."

"But I knew none of them."

"Look at the picture."

"It's hard to see, this picture is destroyed."

"Then ask us questions."

"All right. Shall we?"

"Yes."

"Did he have blue eyes?"

"I remember light eyes."

"And the hair?"

"Dark."

"Black? Brown? Chestnut?"

"I can't remember."

"Tall? Short?"

"A head taller than me."

"Okay. Average weight? Full? Thin?"

They would burst into tears. "I can't remember. Just pick one."

They wanted their children to be tall like their fathers,

strong like their husbands, wise like their grandfathers, tender like their mothers.

At a loss, she turned to William.

"You can't back out of this," he told her.

"What do you suggest?"

"Randomly pick someone who looks like the patient."

Katrina was dumbstruck. "Randomly?"

"Yes. In most cases, they are idolizing their loved ones. I end up picking for them. All of our donors have been carefully chosen. They couldn't find better options if they tried."

"Are you one of the donors?"

"No."

"Why not? You've got excellent parameters."

"It's got nothing to do with my parameters."

"Does it have to do with your father's past?"

Softly, William said. "It's got nothing to do with anything. I don't want to get into it."

"Did you never want children of your own?"

"No."

A**fter** Katrina's first court testimony, an article on the front page of *The New York Times* stated that, "While von Antrim walked up to the stand as if to a gallows, Katrina took the stand like an award winner climbing up on stage, her smile tyrannical, prepared to defend von Antrim with her own body, absorb every one of Goldstone's aggressive questions, and strike back with a lethal blow."

About Goldstone, the article said, "the old lion looked sicker and more tired than ever, as if determined to die on the courtroom floor as the indicting gavel blows echoed between the walls in a glorious, macabre requiem."

Erica's tears left Katrina expressionless. But when Goldstone made William bury his face in his hands and confess his father's crimes with a broken voice, her frozen mask cracked and she took the stand with a murderous countenance.

"How did you meet the defendant?"

"We didn't. William is my cousin. We grew up together in the family mansion until the day he left."

"A maternal or paternal cousin?"

"Paternal."

"How many years did you live together?"

"He was seven years old when he went to America."

"How would you describe your relationship?"

"Very close. Of all the cousins I grew up with, he and I had the most meaningful connection."

"What is the age difference between you?"

"Five years."

"When was the next time you saw him after he left for America?"

"When he came to the reading of our grandmother's will. She asked that her will be read while she was still alive."

"So in spite of your close connection as children, in reality you fell out of touch for many years."

"During the war, any contact between us could have put William and his mother at risk. As far as the American immigration authorities were concerned, they were citizens of an enemy country, and—"

"I'm asking about the period after the war. Germany is now the United States' most loyal European ally. You and the rest of the family had ample opportunity to ask him to return to Germany, but you didn't. My question is: why?"

Katrina was tentative. "Some people in our family had trouble accepting William as the legitimate inheritor."

Goldstone stood up, leaning a hand against the table. "Did you have any trouble accepting General von Antrim's son as the family successor?"

Katrina moistened her lips. "I didn't. In fact, I thought he was the worthiest among us."

"Who then?"

"My uncle Hans had a hard time," the words shot out

of her mouth. "After William's father was killed, Hans saw himself as the natural successor. He and his sons."

"This is Uncle Hans the entomologist, the defendant's father's younger brother?"

"Correct."

"Why did he think his sons were worthier successors? Were they not intellectually impaired?"

"And yet he did."

"Why?"

"Because they were Aryan."

Goldstone turned to face the jury. "Aryan, purebred, but retarded..." Then he whipped his head back toward Katrina. "And you, ma'am? Did you ever think your uncle was correct?"

"No!"

"Even when you considered how the mansion, the many possessions, an ancient noble title, a dynasty reaching back all the way to Frederick Barbarossa, may all fall into the hands of a Jew?"

"William isn't Jewish."

"What about the letter from the Gestapo claiming that William and his mother are Jewish?"

"A fake," she said confidently. "It's no secret that the Gestapo employed the greatest forgers in the country. They used forged documents to get rid of political opponents."

"Who knew the letter had been forged?"

"Grandmother. The families had been marrying each other for generations. They were perfectly Aryan."

"Why then did she not advise them to stay in Germany?"

"She thought it was a fine opportunity to save them, and that America was the safest place for William."

"Who do you think forged the letter?"

"I don't know."

"Can you venture a guess as to who would have an interest in doing so?"

"Your honor," said Blumenthal, "the witness already stated she didn't know."

"Sustained."

Goldstone lowered his head. "Your honor, last night we obtained some documents that might shed new light on this affair. I would like—"

"Objection, your honor," Blumenthal interjected. "Since these documents have not been presented to the defense as required by law and may cause severe harm to the defense, I demand that the jury disregard them. Alternatively, I request that this session be ended right away in order to allow us time to review the new documents and amend the writ of defense accordingly."

Goldstone looked away. "Your honor, we received Gestapo documents from the military archive in Saint Petersburg last night. Suffice it to say that the archive is open to anyone, including my honorable colleague. At any rate, these documents raise severe concerns about the witness's good faith."

The judge gestured for Goldstone to approach the bench. "I hope you appreciate what I'm doing for you," he whispered in the attorney's ear. "View it as a parting gesture. But, for your own sake, don't push it." Then, louder, he announced, "The witness will answer the question."

"Like I said," Katrina replied, "I don't know."

Goldstone placed the document before her. "Have you ever seen this?"

Katrina pulled out her reading glasses and perused the documents without showing any emotion. "I've never seen this before."

Goldstone took the document from her. "Allow me to translate it for the court. The official translation is also filed as a legal exhibit." He cleared his throat. "'On March 4th, 1938, Hauptsturmführer Hans Joachim von Antrim reported to his direct commander that, according to his thorough research, Ms. Eva Hildegard Lisabetta Wittgenstein had a great-grandmother of Jewish descent, and therefore, on the basis of reliable evidence, she is considered a second degree *mischling*." Goldstone paused, taking a step closer to Katrina. "Were you aware that Hans had reported this information?"

Katrina glanced at William.

Louder, Goldstone said, "Ma'am, please answer the question."

"We didn't know," Katrina said. "Well, we knew, but... not at first, anyway... Hans was furious. He claimed he should have been his brother's legal successor. When he was nearing the end of his life and heavily medicated, he told us about tipping off the Gestapo. By that point, it was too late for William."

"Why didn't you tell William and his mother about Hans's actions?"

"My grandmother didn't want to cause a rift in the family."

"Was it after Hans passed away that you decided to become involved in William's project?"

"Yes. I decided to contribute to it long after Hans died."

"What inspired your decision?"

"I read about the project in the newspaper and resonated with his intentions completely."

"Meaning, you resonated with the idea of fertilizing Jewish survivors of Nazi death camps with the sperm of the son of a convicted Nazi criminal?"

"Objection, your honor! The prosecution—"

The judge pounded his gavel. "Sustained. This is your final warning, Mr. Goldstone. Next time, I will put the examination on hold until you submit all your questions to me for review."

Goldstone moved on. "I imagine when you read the newspaper article you realized these were Jewish survivors of the extermination camps?"

"Yes. I resonated with his choice to help these women have children. The fact that they are survivors or that they are Jewish played no role in my decision."

"Meaning, you were not motivated by guilt?"

"No. I empathized with a woman's need to procreate."

"As a German, don't you feel some guilt toward these women?"

Blumenthal approached the bench. "Your honor, we must put an end to this. The witness's emotions have no impact on the actions attributed to my client."

Goldstone addressed the judge. "Your honor, during the war, the company owned by the witness and her late husband produced parts for tanks, jets, train cars, and train tracks in service of the Wehrmacht. This alone raises great doubts about the witness's intentions toward the survivors."

"Overruled. The prosecutor shall repeat the question."

"Would it be correct to assume that your desire to help William and the survivors was motivated by guilt?"

Katrina smiled sarcastically. "I sleep well at night, if that's what you mean."

Goldstone glared at her. "Did you sleep well at night knowing that tens of millions of men, women, and children were murdered and tortured, having been carried to their own private infernos across train tracks made by Mayer and Hedwig Inc.?"

Blumenthal stood up. "Your honor, these allegations are not backed by evidence. The witness cannot be held responsible for the use the Nazi regime made of her steel parts."

"Your honor," Goldstone said, "the prosecution is attempting to prove that the same anti-Semitic motives that led the witness to sell steel to the German death industry also inspired her to impregnate Jewish women with a sperm donation from the son of an S.S. officer."

The judge looked at the witness. "Please answer the question."

Katrina turned to face the jury. "We were forced to sign the contracts," she explained. "If we didn't, the factory would have continued to produce steel parts using forced labor. No power in the world could have stopped the Nazi party."

"But you could have slowed down," Goldstone said. "You could have sabotaged the machines or the assembly lines. We have an urgent letter sent by your floor managers to the company headquarters, in which they ask for increased manpower in order to meet deadlines."

"These floor managers were party members appointed by the Wehrmacht. They were the de-facto factory heads. Herman, my late husband, served merely as a rubber stamp at that point."

Goldstone placed another piece of paper in front of Katrina. "Would you please tell the court what this document is?"

Katrina looked it over. "This is a merger contract, between the company I owned and the company Herman owned."

"Do you recognize the name of the attorney whose signature appears on this agreement?"

"Yes."

"Would you please state her name for the court?"

"It's the plaintiff, Erica Abbet."

"Is that a coincidence?"

"Not at all. Abbet Attorneys was one of the best law firms dealing with mergers in companies of our magnitude. In fact, it was the most famous one."

"And the close ties Abbet had with the Nazi party leadership were not a factor when choosing this law firm?"

"Of course they were. This merger was made for the purpose of a big military bid. Abbet's contacts helped speed up bureaucracy."

"So you decided to go ahead with the merger in order to perform your transaction with the Wehrmacht. You wanted this collaboration."

"We certainly wanted the bid. It was survival as far as we were concerned. If we didn't seal the deal, our factories would have been nationalized."

"So in order to survive, you signed a deal with the devil."

Katrina's lips twisted into a bitter smile. "We supplied steel," she said defiantly.

Goldstone took a step back. "Did you know the plaintiff at the time?"

"A superficial acquaintance. She attended meetings as an advisor, and the negotiation between the companies was mediated by her husband."

"Did you know she was Jewish?"

"No. Her husband was a senior member of the Nazi party. It never occurred to me she might be Jewish."

"When did you find out?"

"The day after we signed the final merger agreement, when I called to ask for copies. The office manager informed me that Abbet had been taken in for an interrogation at the Gestapo headquarters."

"Do you know whose sperm donation was used to impregnate the plaintiff?"

"It was a German donor."

"I imagine your records include the donor's information as well as the patient's?"

"Of course."

"Who performed the fertilization?"

"We have several doctors who do that."

"Who performed them on Jewish refugees?"

"Most often, Dr. von Antrim."

"Does the performing doctor know the source of the donation when they perform it?"

"Each patient's personal file includes all the details. The donor's identity appears in code."

"Did Dr. von Antrim know the plaintiff was fertilized with his own sperm?"

Katrina's face tightened. "I don't know," she said drily. "Most doctors don't bother to check."

"Did he or did he not?"

Blumenthal raised his hand. "Objection. The witness already answered very clearly that she does not know whether my client was aware of the donor's identity at the time of the procedure."

"Your honor," said Goldstone, "in her deposition, the witness stated that she was the one who'd prepared Dr. von Antrim's donation for the plaintiff, and that Dr. von Antrim had been the one to perform the procedure."

The judge hit his gavel. "Overruled. The witness will answer the question."

"The plaintiff received Dr. von Antrim's donation," said Katrina.

"And what about the other Jewish women? Whose donations did they receive?"

Katrina closed her eyes.

"Ma'am," said the judge, "please answer the question."

Katrina opened her eyes and gave Goldstone a hateful stare. "Dr. von Antrim's," she spat. "Only Dr. von Antrim's."

Goldstone felt dizzy. His knees buckled and he collapsed into his seat.

"Are you able to carry on, Mr. Goldstone?" asked the judge.

"I'm not feeling well, your honor. Motion to continue my examination tomorrow."

The judge pounded his gavel and court was adjourned.

That evening, William found Katrina asleep in the living room, her body splayed out on the large sofa, her hair wild, her mouth gaping open. Her breathing was heavy and wheezing. Black eyeliner streamed down her face, forging grooves through her skin. From time to time, an agonized sigh disturbed her peace, and a sudden tremble shook her body. She mumbled something unintelligible, her face twisting with pain, then fell deeper into sleep again. A half-empty bottle of whiskey was lying on the floor, and the shards of a crystal glass were scattered over the rug.

William kneeled and carefully collected the shards.

Suddenly, she opened her eyes. Noticing William, she sat up slowly. "You're back?"

"I'm back."

"I spoiled everything for you," she said, her voice hollow.

"You spoiled nothing."

"I spoiled everything."

"It's fine. I'll make you some strong coffee."

Katrina tried to get up, but her head was spinning and she fell back onto the sofa.

From the kitchen, William called, "Be careful, the floor is covered with glass. Don't walk around barefoot."

She nudged her feet into slippers and held her arms out. "Help me up? There's food in the oven. You must be starving."

He helped her take a seat by the table and went into the kitchen. When he returned, she was filling her glass with wine. "I think we've had enough to drink," he remarked.

Katrina made a face. "Speak for yourself."

He corked the bottle and returned it to the sideboard. Katrina downed her wine in a single gulp, then slammed the glass back on the table. "Give me back the bottle," she ordered him. "I'm not your child."

William began piling pot roast, baked potatoes, and salad onto her plate. "You've had a rough day," he said tenderly. "You need a good meal and a good night's sleep. You're going back on the stand again tomorrow."

Katrina laughed recklessly. "Don't worry," she said, out of breath. "I'll take proper care of that Goldstone tomorrow."

William put the plate in front of her. "Blumenthal asked to meet with you early tomorrow morning to prepare you for the testimony. He said it's very important."

Katrina shook her head vigorously. "I don't need any preparation." When she finished eating she walked to the sideboard and poured herself another glass of wine. She downed it and poured another, then swayed around the room. "So, William? Scruples!"

"What are you talking about?"

Katrina leaned against the wall and laughed, wine splashing from her glass. "Your grandiose project, my darling."

William took the glass from her shaky hand and sat her down in the armchair.

"Don't take my wine, please."

"I'm just setting it down for you."

Katrina picked up the glass and gulped with pleasure. "Do you see, my darling?" she murmured. "Us Germans do well with pangs of conscience. We get them at regular intervals, like goddamn menstruation. First we annihilate, and then we cry. The good news is, we get over it within a few years. But when we lose our minds—God save us from ourselves." She gestured toward him, glass in hand. "Just look at yourself," she chided. "Anyone can see you're in agony."

William looked up from his plate, smiling lovingly at her. Katrina was certainly unique. Direct, emotional, but simultaneously as hard and cutting as a steel cord.

"I'm not talking about all the millions of dollars you're wasting," she said angrily. "I'm talking about your insane sacrifice, your miserable life. Don't you think it's something we need to resolve?"

William slowly wiped the corner of his mouth with a napkin. "Of course we do. Got any interesting ideas for me?"

She lifted the hand holding the glass. "I've got an excellent idea."

"I'm all ears."

"What's needed here is some balance. Call it symmetrical justice. One German for each Jewish victim. That's fair, right? How many do they claim we exterminated? Five? Six million? We'll give them six million Germans to exterminate. An eye for an eye. We can scrounge up six million superfluous Germans like nothing. We've got lists, thank goodness. But we'll give the young ones another chance at life first, won't we?"

William nodded in overarching agreement. "Of course we will."

She sipped her wine and wiped her mouth with her hand. "We've got to. They're young. They can still change, can't they? At any rate, I suggest we start with the old, the infirm, the war veterans. Some of them would pounce at the opportunity. Instead of rotting to death in a geriatric ward, they'd die a hero's death. What could be better? Any old Nazi fart with Parkinson's and a cancerous prostate would much rather end his life with an Israeli soldier's bullet in his head. Just before they take him out, we'll let him laugh like a lunatic, scream '*Heil* Hitler!' He'll rave to the soldier, 'I murdered your grandfather! I fucked your grandmother!' before he takes a bullet between the eyes."

William pursed his lips, impressed. "Not bad, Kati. Not bad at all."

Another sip for good measure, and she stood up. "Wait a minute, wait a minute, listen," she said softly, secretively. "The Israelis actually won't have to kill the Germans right away, not while they're still useful. We turned the Jews into soap, lampshades, bulbs. They can turn our Nazis into human lab rats to be used in their military industry, in pharmaceutical companies. They can use them to test new medications, intended to ease the lives of survivors. How's that for poetic justice?"

She began pacing again, swaying in broken circles, head tilted forward, eyes fixed on a point high up in the space of the room. "Hang on, I've got another idea. What do you think about testing the endurance of the human body in nuclear explosions, its ability to absorb radioactive radiation? What do you think?" She burst out laughing. "Oh, but one couldn't come up with worse mutations than what we already are."

"Fantastic, fantastic, Kati. Let's save some ideas for tomorrow. Time for bed now."

Katrina lit a cigarette and puffed on it gluttonously. "Are you listening?"

"I'm all ears."

"All right. We could use the ashes for organic fertilizers. Compost, heaps of compost. Imagine what that's going to do for Israeli agriculture! The orchards! The flavor of their oranges would certainly improve. They'd be able to export them to Germany. We'd pay full price, just to be clear."

"Of course. Full price. Now let's go to sleep."

Tears began to stream down her face. Her speech turned muddled and muffled. She started toward the bedroom. "I'm not drunk, William, I'm... I'm... By the way, that whiskey bottle was nearly empty when I found it. I just... I needed something strong to perk me up after what I've been through today. Do you understand?"

"Completely."

"I'm just worried about you, William."

"I know."

She turned her stained face toward him. Voice cracked, she cried, "The hell they're putting you through!"

Flatly, William said, "They aren't doing anything to me, Katrina."

Her eyes rounded with marvel. "Nothing?"

"Nothing. It's simply my fate."

The next morning, Goldstone felt a hint of that sneaky emotion people call happiness. Warmth filled his chest as he watched his three sons sitting in the front row, smiling at him lovingly. He removed his foggy glasses, blew his nose noisily, and surreptitiously wiped his tears away. Their presence bolstered him, yet also made him fret. Losing was out of the question in this case. The German doctor must receive a life sentence. Had the death sentence been available to Goldstone, he would have pursued it without hesitation.

The judge gestured for him to begin.

"What was your position in Dr. von Antrim's project?"

"I advised patients in choosing a donor," said Katrina.

"All patients?"

"Mostly the Jewish ones."

"Why is that?"

"Most of them spoke German."

"And beyond consultations, these women received financial aid throughout pregnancy, correct?"

"Only the Jewish refugees did."

"Why is that?"

"As refugees, they were not entitled to the kind of subsidized medical insurance that covers IVF. Besides, their finances were bad."

"What was the source of your funding?"

"William covered the cost out of his personal wealth, and there were also some donations from different organizations. Later on, we used the payments made by American patients to cover the cost of caring for the refugees. We've got a large group of Evangelical donors, but the vast majority of donations comes from Germany."

"So you approached German donors?"

"We approached no one. The German donations started coming in after an article about William's project was published in a German newspaper."

"The same article that led you to move here and join his project?"

"That's right."

"And who are these donors?"

"I have no idea. The funds were transferred directly into the bank account we posted in the media."

"How much money are we talking about? Thousands? Hundreds of thousands? Millions?"

"I have no idea. Our bookkeeper would be able to give you a precise answer."

"Ballpark?"

Blumenthal said, "Objection, your honor. The witness already stated she does not know the answer."

"Sustained."

"Did you try to get in touch with them?"

Katrina glanced at the jury. "No, most of the donations were anonymous."

"Don't you think that's strange? So soon after the war, such a flow of donations from Germany?"

"Some people have a conscience," Katrina offered, "even in Germany."

Goldstone limped toward the witness stand, where he leaned closer to Katrina. "Might some of your donors be Nazis?"

"Why would a Nazi pay money to bring more Jewish babies into the world?"

"Have you heard about Professor Irving Haberkamp's research?" he asked.

"No."

"Well, Professor Haberkamp, a world-renowned sociologist, claims that Neo-Nazi groups have undergone a transformation with regards to their perception of how to resolve 'the Jewish problem.' In the past, they subscribed to the physical extinction of Jews—an enterprise which eventually failed. Nowadays, the working theory is that absolute genetic extinction of the Jewish people can be attained by what they call 'genetic dilution'—the invasion of a foreign dominant genome into the Jewish genome. This isn't exactly a novel idea. Many peoples have assimilated into other populations and disappeared from the face of history in this way."

"What is your question?" Katrina asked.

"As an international expert on molecular genetics, wouldn't you say that implanting a German man's DNA into the wombs of Jewish women is an attempt at assimilation and the dilution of the Jewish genetic pool?"

"Objection, your honor," Blumenthal barked. "This is a deranged theory devoid of any scientific foundation. I ask that your honor reject this question."

"Your honor," Goldstone cut in, "it is on the basis of such pseudo-scientific theories that, in August 1936, the Nazis started the first Lebensborn home of their racial purity program in the village of Steinhöring, near Munich. Thirty-seven similar centers were later opened all across Europe, where close to 16,000 'genetically improved children' were born. We have verified documentation of Nazi organizations that regularly donate to laboratories dealing with genetic engineering."

The judge pounded his gavel. "Overruled."

Katrina flushed. "We didn't check the donors' political affiliation. For the sake of these miserable women, we were willing to take money even from the devil himself."

Goldstone smiled venomously. "This, from the woman who signed commercial contracts with the devil to the tune of millions of marks."

"Your honor, it is preposterous—"

The judge hit the gavel. "Mr. Goldstone, I believe we have exhausted this line of questioning. Do you have anything to add?"

"Yes, sir."

"Please, get to the point."

Goldstone nodded. "Why did you decide to fertilize the Jewish refugees exclusively with von Antrim's sperm?"

"William is an ideal donor in every way."

He leaned in. "How many pregnancies were attained from the defendant's donations?"

"I can't remember exactly."

"You claimed to have exact records. Give me an approximate figure. Hundreds? Thousands? Tens of thousands?"

"A few thousand."

"How many thousands, give or take?"

"About six thousand."

"According to your deposition, you prepared the donations for Jewish patients yourself. Meaning, you are directly responsible for impregnating them with German sperm, correct?"

"As long as the donor wasn't Jewish, I don't see the problem."

"Still, this is German sperm."

Katrina smirked. "Like I said, there must be some good Germans out there after all."

Goldstone pointed at William accusingly. "This good German's father was an indicted mass murderer."

Katrina's voice sharpened as she shifted a tyrannical gaze toward the jury. "I implanted them with the DNA of a highly moral, generous, well-educated, handsome, able-bodied, and able-minded man. And I can prove it," she added.

Goldstone's eyes narrowed into two slits of loathing. "Prove what?"

Katrina rested her palm on the stack of papers in front of her. "I have irrefutable proof here that William's donations created good Jews, physically and psychologically healthy, down to the last one."

Blumenthal got up, his face pale. He read the scheme all over her face. "Your honor," he said, his voice shaking, "the witness is acting in complete opposition to my legal counsel. She has no proof, and I ask that her remark be stricken from the court records."

The judge's voice hardened. "Mr. Blumenthal," he fumed, "may I remind you that the witness is currently under cross-examination. I won't allow you to disturb the process." Then he turned to Goldstone. "You may proceed."

A sharp pain erupted in Goldstone's temples. He sat down and breathed heavily. Then his distorted face loosened. "Absolutely," he said meekly. "I would love to hear your scientific proof."

The judge turned to Katrina. "Ma'am, you may present your proof."

Blumenthal hurried over to the bench. "Your honor," he said softly, "the witness has made it her goal to hurt the prosecutor personally."

The judge flushed. "Mr. Blumenthal, you have been repeatedly disrupting cross-examination. I'll ask that you kindly take your seat."

"Your honor, my witness intends to break medical confidentiality."

"Well, then, I suppose the prosecutor will deal with this in his own way." The judge turned to Katrina again. "Please carry on."

Katrina placed her hand on the stack of papers again. "My proof is based on the analysis of thousands of follow-up visits Dr. von Antrim conducted with the children of Jewish refugees conceived through in-vitro. His examinations tested their physical and mental health, along with how they fit in with their peers, their academic accomplishments, and, later on, their marriages and professional careers. The results teach us that the rate of physical and mental illness in these offspring is significantly lower than among their peers. I also analyzed a sample of the first thirty Jewish patients ever impregnated with Dr. von Antrim's sperm, over twenty-five years ago, so the results offer a clear image of William's donation quality.

"Take for instance, the file of patient GE-6701-W1-1/4. You can see that the woman—"

Things happened quickly after that. Blumenthal pounced at Katrina, took hold of the stack of papers, and began ripping them to shreds.

"Mr. Blumenthal!" the judge roared. "I ask you to leave this courtroom immediately and wait for me in my chambers. I must say, I am shocked by this outburst. I hope you have a satisfactory explanation. Court will resume in one hour, exactly." He motioned to two ushers standing in the doorway. They hurried over, quickly gathered the scattered paper shreds, and placed them in a pile on the stand.

Katrina slipped on her glasses and began to rearrange the papers.

When the session resumed, Goldstone wasn't feeling well. His headache was getting worse. The figures in the courtroom spun before his eyes, faceless. His left cheek was numb. Nauseous, he sipped from the glass of water on the table.

"Your witness, Mr. Goldstone," said the judge.

Goldstone limped toward the witness stand. "You

were about to show us proof from a specific patient's file. What is unique about this patient?"

Scorched by his proximity, by the distilled radiation of his agony, by the warm breath of his hate, Katrina raised her head from the stack of documents and glanced at Goldstone through her reading glasses. "She was one of our first patients," she said, her smile tender. "A beautiful woman, and amiable. A theatre actress, if I'm not mistaken. She cried so much when she discovered her husband was barren. She told Dr. von Antrim that her husband was the sole survivor of his entire family."

"I still don't see any proof of..." he trailed off as a sharp pain sliced through his temples and grabbed the stand, spasming. "What's special about her?" he mumbled, wheezing. "What's special about this woman?"

Katrina's gray eyes widened. Her thin lips curled into a toxic smile. Raising her voice, she said, "Mrs. Ida Goldstone, patient GE-6701-W1-1/4 had three children, all conceived exclusively with Dr. von Antrim's sperm donation. At her final visit to the clinic, she told us that she and her husband were overjoyed. They had smart, healthy, well-behaved children, all gifted with a warm Jewish heart. Not a drop of malice in their blood."

Goldstone's cause of death remains a mystery; a medical "non liquet" which would likely never be resolved. The doctors could not determine whether a stroke and a massive brain hemorrhage caused him to fall, or whether falling on the corner of the witness stand and hitting the base of his skull led him to suffer a stroke. Either way, the malignant cancer in his lungs, as metastasized as it may have been, was not even considered as a cause of death following autopsy results. If Goldstone could have heard this, he would have taken vengeful pleasure in knowing that, in death, he'd finally beaten his cancer.

He spent three days in the ICU. Two NYPD officers blocked the entrance to his hospital room, keeping out scandal-thirsty journalists and photographers. A chilly silence filled the room. Monitors counted time as it ran out with metallic taps and beeps. Drops of clear plasma dripped through the I.V., keeping pace. The nurses slipped colorful tubes into his open mouth.

Goldstone's eyes, round and empty, stared at the ceiling with the same stunned expression he'd had when he shifted his gaze from his sons to Dr. von Antrim, from Dr. von Antrim to Katrina, and back again. He had the same look in his eyes as he was lowered into his grave.

Printed in Great Britain
by Amazon